Kalidas

Shakuntala

Or, the lost ring. A melo drama, in seven acts

Kalidas

Shakuntala
Or, the lost ring. A melo drama, in seven acts

ISBN/EAN: 9783337344429

Printed in Europe, USA, Canada, Australia, Japan

Cover: Foto ©Andreas Hilbeck / pixelio.de

More available books at **www.hansebooks.com**

ŚHAKUNTALÀ.

OR

THE LOST RING.

A Melo Drama,

IN SEVEN ACTS,

BY

KALIDAS.

Bombay:

PRINTED AT THE "ROYAL PRESS."

1867.

Cast of the Characters.

As performed for the first time by the Kalidas Elphinstone Society, at the Grant Road Theatre Bombay, on Saturday the 19th October 1867.

Dushyanta,—*King of India*, ...Mr. B. V. N. KIRTIKAR.

Mathavya,—*The jester, friend and companion of the King* .... „ B. D. TALPADE.

Kanwa,—*Chief of the hermits, foster-father of Shakuntala,*...... „ V. M. TRILOKEKAR.

Sharngarava,—*A Brahman, belonging to the hermitage of Kanwa*... „ G. B. VIJAYAKAR.

Sharadwata,—Do. do. ... „ B. K. DESAI.

Mitravasu,—*Brother-in-law of the King and Superintendent of the City Police,*..................... „ M. R. TALPADE.

Januka,—*A Constable,* .... „ V. V. R. JAYAKAR.

Suchaka,—Do. do. .... „ B. K. DESAI.

Vatayana,—*The chamberlain or attendant on the women's apartments,* „ D. M. VIJAYAKAR.

Somarata,—*The domestic priest,* ... „ G. M. ZAOBA.

Charioteer,—*To the King,* .... „ G. B. VIJAYAKAR.

Karabhaka,—*A messenger of the queen-mother,*........................ „ G. M. ZAOBA.

Raivatika,—*The warder or door-keeper,* .... „ R. V. A. DHAIRYAVAN.

Fisherman,—*Of Shakravatar,*...... „ B. T. R. RANJIT.

Matali,—*Charioteer of Indra* ...... „ R. V. A. DHAIRYAVAN.

Sarva-Damana,—*Afterwards named Bharata, (a little boy,) son of Dushyanta by Shakuntala,* ...... „ J. F. MANKAR.

Kashyapa,—*A divine sage, progenitor of men and gods, son of Marichi, and grandson of Brahma* .... „ R. A. MANKAR.

Vykhanas,—*A disciple of Kanva,* „ B. K. DESAI.

Shakuntala,—*Daughter of the sage Vishvamitra and the Nymph Menaka, foster child of the hermit Kanwa*................................. „ A. F. MANKAR.

Priyamvada,—*Female attendant, companion of Shakuntala*.......... „ V. S. DHARADHAR.

Anasuya,—Do. do. ...... „ R. B. VIJAYAKAR.

Gautami,—*A holy matron, superior of the female inhabitants of the hermitage,* .... „ S. B. Vijayakar.

Parabaritika,—*Maiden in charge of the royal gardens,* .... „ R. G. Pradhan.

Madhukarika,—Do. do. ... „ R. K. Desai.

Aditi,—*Wife of Kashyapa grand-mother of Brahma, through her father Daksha* .... „ S. B. Mankar.

Officers, attendants, Yavan women, and Hermits.

Scene—During a greater part of the play in a first on the Banks of the Malini in India and sometimes at Hastanapur (the modern Delhi.)

Programme of the Scenery.

Act I. Scene I.—A Forest. An hermitage in the centre, elastic turf, Bowers of creepers. Plantations of cane and Plantain trees.

Act II. Scene I.—A plain on the skirts of the forest, a rock in the centre.

Act III. Scene I.—The sacred grove.

Act IV. Scene I.—The hermitage in the centre. Scene II. A room in the hermitage. A sacrificial fire burning in the centre. A group of hermits differently occupied.

Act V. Scene I.—A room in the Palace. The King's throne in the centre. Shakuntala carried up in the heavens. Stage dark. Geen, blue and red lights. A grand Tableau.

Act VI.—Prelude. Scene I.—A Street. Scene II.— Frontage of the Palace with centre door.

Act VI. Scene I,—The garden of the Palace. Fountain playing in the centre, surrounded by gas light buckets. Flower pots. Garden seats, and other available embellishments. The car of Indra descending and ascending.

Act VII. Scene I.—The sky. Car of Indra moving in the clouds. Ditto descending. Scene II.—The sacred grove of Kashyapa.

Costume.

———◆———

DUSHYANTA—*First Dress.*—Rich embroidered Punjabi
coat, trowsers to match, gold laced feta for the
head with shirpecha, stockings, embroidered shoes,
wristlets, armlets, necklaces, bow, arrow and
quiver. *Second dress—Mourning.*—Plain white
feta, ditto coat, trowsers to match, shoes, stockings.
Third dress—Court.—Glittering embroidered Punjabi coat, trowsers to match, rich valuable tiara set
in emeralds and rubies, stockings, embroidered shoes,
wristlets, armlets, necklaces (pearl and gold) bow, arrow, and quiver.

MATHAVYA.—Fantastic Punch like conical shaped hat
with jingling bells and peacock feathers. Comic
coat with a freize of jingling bells, trousers to match,
stockings (one red strapped another white) shoes
(one Bramhan fashion and another Punjabi) a staff
(a branch of a tree).

KANVA.—Silvery long hair, silvery long beard, body covered with ashes, great blanket robe, sandals, tiger skin,
wand, Rudraksha necklaces and Rudraksha earrings.

OTHER HERMITS.—A crown of Rudraksha over the head,
grey or black long hair, grey or black long beard,
a blanket or madder coloured robe, sandals, wand,
body covered with ashes, tiger or deer skin, Gowmu-
khi, (L shaped bag) asanvati rudraksha necklaces.

MITRAVASU.—Plain Punjabi feta, plain Punjabi long coat,
trousers to match, long moustach, stockings and shoes,
and a bludgeon, sword and sash.

CONSTABLES.—Marathi fashioned turbands, plain coats,
plain trousers, Punjabi common shoes, swords.

CHAMBERLAIN.—Punjabi plain feta, grey long beard,
large staff, Punjabi plain coat, trousers, plain Punjabi
shoes.

DOMESTIC PRIEST.—Bramhan's cap, beard, rich embroidered shawl, Nagpur silk bordered dhotar,

silver panchpatri and pali, silver snuff box and copy
of a native almanak (Panchang.)

CHARIOTEER.—A Punjabi feta, coat, trousers, whip
and sash.

KARABHAK. Ditto.

RAIVATIKA. Ditto.

FISHERMAN.—Fisherman's cap, ditto langoti, silver w aist
band, knife suspending on the breast, hooks, nets
and angles

MATALI.—Rich glittering crown, rich glittering spangled
coat, brocaded trousers.

SARVA-DAMAN.—A Cashmere cap, ditto zabla, and trouser
with an amulet and a puppy.

SHAKUNTALA.—*First dress*—bark bodice, ditto sarree,
nose-ring, head ornaments. *Second dress*—rich glittering Benares sarree, bodice to match, bangles, wirstlets,
armlets, pearl and gold necklaces, head ornaments,
earrings, nose-ring, anklets. *Third dress*—Plain
white saree, bodice to match, hair twisted in a long
braid.

PRIYAMVADA *and* ANASUYA.—See Shakuntala's first
dress.

GOUTAMI *and* ADITI. Grey hair and matronly Hindu
lady's plain dress

PARABARITIKA *and* MADHUKARIKA.—Hindu Maiden's
plain dress.

Music.

ACT I.

1st Que.—Rising of the curtain. ...	Hunting Horn (outside.)
2nd Que.—The King is obeyed carriage drives off.	Horn again till it re-enters.
3rd Que.—On the King entering the Hermitage.	Soft adajio ad libitum 3 bars.
4th Que.—All sit down on bank . .	3 Chords soft adajio.
5th Que.—Offers a King to Maiden.	3 bars do.
6th Que.—Maidens leaving the stage till gone off ...	Piano tender adajio.
7th Que.—King leaves the stage ...	Melancholy music.

ACT II. V.

1st Que.—King enters accompanied by women ... ... } Horns.

2nd Que.—Come along then (they
sit) ... ... } 3 bars adajio.

ACT III.

1st Que.—King enters (as if in love) Soft serious music 4 bars.

2nd Que.—Three Maidens on a
rock with fans ... } Tender music 3 bars.

3rd Que.—Bound to respect rises
to go... ... ... } One chord.

4th Que.— Let me go. Let me go ... 3 bars hurry.

5th Que.—A voice in the air thunder and lightening. } Full band crash.

6th Que.—I come to the rescue, I   Full band. Hurried Mar-
come ... ...   tial music.

ACT IV.

1st Que.—Two Hermits enter
with presents. ... } 2 Chords.

2nd Que.—Putting on the two
linen mantles ... } 2 Chords.

3rd Que.—Kanwa enters... ... Slow symphony.

4th Que.—Walking round fire ... Piano symphony.

5th Que.—And thy friends kneel-
ing down ... ... } 2 bars symphony.

6th Que.—Kanwa goes out ... 2 bars slow.

V.

1st Que.—King leaves stage ... Trumpet.

2nd Que.—King enters ... ... Do.

3rd Que.—Feeling finger for Ring. One bar surprise.

4th Que.—Receive me in thy bo-
som... ... ... } Slow solemn music till in
clouds.

5th Que.—A miracle, A miracle... Full band. Grand Bursts.

VI.

1st Que.—King enters ... ... Trumpet outside.

2nd Que.—King walking slow up
and down stage ... } Piano serious adajio.

3rd Que.—Car descends ... ... Slow symphony.

4th Que.—Car ascends ... ... Symphony.

VII.

1st Que.—Car floating in sky ... Symphony.

2nd Que.—Touch it not for your
life ... ... } One chord of Surprise.

3rd Que.—Joy ! Joy ! ... ... One chord lively.

SCENE 2nd.—Kashyapa discovered Full band. Sacred music.

Curtain. Grand Tableau. Full band. Harmony.

PREFACE.

In presenting the following pages (more a reprint than an original) to the reading world—the Society do not consider it prudent to expatiate on the merits of the work in these prefatory remarks being so universally known. They only take the liberty to state the reasons which prompted them to republish, though not entirely, a text which has appeared in more than one shape. The merits of the work as a play being too high, and knowing that it had never been put upon any stage, the Society thought of abridging the version of Professor Monier Williams, and putting it in a convenient form after the manner of Lacy's Acting Editions. This being their first attempt and the time at their command being too short, several clerical blunders have inadvertantly crept into the brochure for which they beg to be excused.

The Society embrace this opportunity of publicly testifying to the unremitting exertions of one of their number Mr. R. V. A. Dhairyavan in designing the blocks and superintending over other artistic work.

In conclusion, the Society sanguinely hope that their efforts to please the public will meet with due encouragement at the hands of the discerning public.

The Argument.

"The scence opens with King Dushyanta's hunting excursion in the forest, when he beholds the beautiful Shakuntala, the daughter of Kanwa, the sage ; and he prevails on the damsel to become his wife by a Gandaharva marriage, and gives her his ring as the pledge of his troth. Then Dushyanta returns to his own city, whilst Shakuntala remains in the hermitage of her father. After this Durvasa the sage, visits the hermitage of Kanwa, but the thoughts of Shakuntala being fixed upon her husband, she hears not of the approach of the sage. And Durvasa curses the damsel, that she shall be forgotten by the man she loves ; but after a while he relents and promises that the curse shall be removed as soon as Dushyanta sees the ring. When Shakuntala finds that she is with child, she sets off for the palace of her husband ; but on her way she bathes in a sacred pool, and the ring drops from her finger and is lost beneath the waters. When. she reaches the palace of the King, his memory departs from him, and he does not own her to be his wife ; and her mother comes and carries her away to the jungle, and there she gives birth to a son, who is named Bharata. Here, it so happens that a large fish is caught by a fisherman, and the ring of Dushyanta is found in the belly of the fish, and is carried to the King ; Dushyanta sees the ring, and he remembers the beautiful Shakuntala, who had become his wife by a Gandharva marriage. Upon this the King goes into the jungle and sees the boy Bharata sporting with young lions, and setting at nought the lioness that gives them suck ; his heart burns towards the lad ; and presently he beholds the sorrowing Shakuntala, and recognises her as his wife, and Bharata as his son. So he takes Shakuntala and Bharata to pay their respectful visits to the venerable Kashyapa when the sage onounces a benediction upon them.

SHAKUNTALA; OR, THE LOST RING.

ACT I.

SCENE—*A Forest.* An hermitage to the right.

The sound of horns heard. Enter King DUSHYANTA, *v. l. e. armed with a bow and arrow, in a chariot, chasing an antelope, attended by his* CHARIOTEER.

CHAR. *(Looking at the deer, and then at the* KING.)
Great Prince,

When on the antelope I bend my gaze,
And on your Majesty, whose mighty bow
Has its string firmly braced ; before my eyes
The god that wields the trident[1] seems revealed,
Chasing the deer that flies from him in vain.

KING. Charioteer, this fleet antelope has drawn us far
from my attendants. See ! there he runs :

Aye and anon his graceful neck he bends
To cast a glance at the pursuing car ;
And dreading now the swift-descending shaft,
Contracts into itself his slender frame :
About his path, in scattered fragments strewn,
The half-chewed grass falls from his panting mouth ;
See ! in his airy bounds he seems to fly,
And leaves no trace upon th' elastic turf.

(With astonishment.) How now ! swift as is our pursuit
I scarce can see him,

CHAR. Sire, the ground here is full of hollows ; I have therefore drawn in the reins and checked the speed of the chariot. Hence the deer has somewhat gained upon us. Now that we are passing over level ground, we shall have no difficulty in overtaking him.

KING. Loosen the reins, then.

CHAR. The King is obeyed. (*Drives the chariot at full speed.*)

KING. Now, Charioteer, see me kill the deer. (*Takes aim.*)

A VOICE *(within).* Hold, O King ! this deer belongs to our hermitage. Kill it not ! kill it not !

CHAR. (*Listening and looking.*) Great King, some hermits have stationed themselves so as to screen the antelope at the very moment of its coming within range of your arrow.

KING. (*Hastily.*) Then stop the horses.

CHAR. I obey. (*Stops the Chariot.*)

Enter VYKHANAS, *and two other* HERMITS *with him* R.

VYK. (*Raising his hand.*) This deer, O King, belongs to our hermitage. Kill it not ! kill it not !

Can thy steel bolts no meeter quarry find
Than the warm life-blood of a harmless deer ?
Restore, great Prince, thy weapon to its quiver :
More it becomes thy arms to shield the weak,
Than to bring anguish on the innocent.

KING. 'Tis done. (*Replaces the arrow in its quiver.*)

VYK. Worthy is this action of a Prince, the light of Puru's race.[2]

Well does this act befit a Prince like thee,
Right worthy is it of thine ancestry.
Thy guerdon be a son of peerless worth,
Whose wide dominion shall embrace the earth.

BOTH THE OTHER HERMITS. (*Raising their hands.*) May heaven indeed grant thee a son, a sovereign of the earth from sea to sea !

KING. (*Bowing.*) I accept with gratitude a Bráhman's benediction.

VYK. We came hither, mighty Prince, to collect sacrificial wood. Here on the banks of the Máliní you may perceive the hermitage of the great sage Kanwa.³ If other duties require not your presence, deign to enter and accept our hospitality.

KING. Is the Chief of your Society now at home ?

VYK. No ; he has gone to Soma-tírtha⁴ to propitiate Destiny, which threatens his daughter Shakuntalá with some calamity ; but he has commissioned her in his absence to entertain all guests with hospitality.

KING. Good ! I will pay her a visit. She will make me acquainted with the mighty sage's acts of penance and devotion.

VYK. And we will depart on our errand. (*Exit with his companions* R.)

KING. Charioteer, urge on the horses. We will at least purify our souls by a sight of this hallowed retreat.

CHAR. Your Majesty is obeyed. (*Drives the chariot with great velocity* R.)

KING. (*Looking all about him.*) Charioteer, even without being told, I should have known that these were the precincts of a grove consecrated to penitential rites. (*Advancing a little further.*) The inhabitants of this sacred retreat must not be disturbed. Stay the chariot, that I may alight.

CHAR. The reins are held in. Your Majesty may descend.

KING (*Alighting* R.) Charioteer, groves devoted to penance must be entered in humble attire. Take these ornaments. (*Delivers his ornaments and bow to the* CHARIOTEER.) Charioteer, see that the horses are watered, and attend to

them until I return from visiting the inhabitants of the hermitage.

CHAR. I will. (*Exit* L.)

KING. (*Walking and looking about.*) Here is the entrance to the hermitage. I will now go in.
(*Entering and feeling a throbbing sensation
in his arm.*)

Serenest peace is in this calm retreat,
By passion's breath unruffled ; what portends
My throbbing arm5 ? Why should it whisper here
Of happy love ? Yet everywhere around us
Stand the closed portals of events unknown.

A VOICE (*within*). This way, my dear companions ;
this way.

KING. (*Listening.*) Hark ! I hear voices to the right
of yonder grove of trees. I will walk in that
direction. (*Walking and looking about.*)
Ah ! here are the maidens of the hermitage
coming this way to water the shrubs, carrying
watering-pots proportioned to their strength.
(*Gazing at them.*) How graceful they look !

In palaces such charms are rarely ours ;
The woodland plants outshine the garden flowers.

I will conceal myself in this shade and watch
them. (*Stands gazing at them.*)

Enter SHAKUNTALA, *with her two female companions,
carrying watering pots to water the shrubs* R. U. E.

SHAK. This way, my dear companions ; this way.

KING. (*aside*) Can this be the daughter of Kanwa ? The
saintly man, though descended from the great
Kashyapa, must be very deficient in judgment to
habituate such a maiden to the life of a recluse.
Well ! concealed behind this tree, I will watch
her without raising her suspicion (*Conceals
himself.*)

SHAK.   Good Anasúyá, Priyamvadá has drawn this bark-
             dress too tightly about my chest. I pray thee,
             loosen it a little.

ANA   I will. (*Loosens it.*)

PRIY.   (*Smiling.*) Why do you lay the blame on me?
             Blame rather your own blooming youthful-
             ness which imparts fulness to your bosom.

KING.   (*aside*) A most just observation!

This youthful form, whose bosom's swelling charms
By the bark's knotted tissue are concealed,
Like some fair bud close folded in its sheath,
Gives not to view the blooming of its beauty.

             But what am I saying? In real truth, this bark-
             dress, though ill-suited to her figure, sets it
             off like an ornament.

PRIY.   Dear Shakuntalá, yon Keshara-tree[6] whilst your
             graceful form bends about its stem, appears as
             if it were wedded to some lovely twining
             creeper.

SHAK.   Ah! saucy girl, you are most appropriately named
             Priyamvadá (' Speaker of flattering things').

KING.   (*Aside.*) What Priyamvadá says, though
             complimentary, is nevertheless true. Verily,

Her ruddy lip vies with the opening bud;
Her graceful arms are as the twining stalks;
And her whole form is radiant with the glow
Of youthful beauty, as the tree with bloom.

ANA.   You see, dear Shakuntalá, here is the young jasmine,
             which you named 'the Moonlight of the
             Grove,' the self-elected wife of the mango-
             tree. Have you forgotten it?

SHAK.   Rather will I forget myself. (*Approaching the
             plant and looking at it.*) How delightful is
             the season when the jasmine-creeper and the
             mango-tree seem thus to unite in mutual em-
             braces! The fresh blossoms of the jasmine
             resemble the bloom of a young bride, and the

newly-formed shoots of the mango appear to make it her natural protector. (*Continues gazing at it.*)

PRIY. (*Smiling.*) Do you know, my Anasúyá, why Shakuntalá gazes so intently at the jasmine ?

ANA. No, indeed, I cannot imagine. I pray thee tell me.

PRIY. She is wishing that as the jasmine is united to a suitable tree, so, in like manner, she may obtain a husband worthy of her.

SHAK. Speak for yourself, girl, this is the thought in your own mind. (*Continues watering the flowers.*)

KING. (*Aside.*) Would that my union with her were permissible ! and yet I hardly dare hope that the maiden is sprung from a caste different from that of the Head of the hermitage. However, come what may, I will ascertain the fact.

SHAK. (*In a flurry.*) Ah ! a bee, disturbed by the sprinkling of the water, has left the young jasmine, and is trying to settle on my face. (*Attempts to drive it away.*)

KING. (*Aside ; Gazing at her ardently.*) Beautiful ! there is something charming even in her repulse. (*In a tone of envy.*)

Ah happy bee ! how boldly dost thou try
To steal the lustre from her sparkling eye.

SHAK. This impertinent bee will not rest quiet. I must move elsewhere. (*Moving a few steps off* L, *and casting a glance around.*) How now ! he is following me here. Help ! my dear friends, help ! deliver me from the attacks of this troublesome insect.

PRIY. How can we deliver you ? Call Dushyanta to your aid. The sacred groves are under the king's special protection.

KING. (*Aside.*) An excellent opportunity for me to show myself. (*Aloud.*) Fear not—(*Checks himself when the words are half-uttered. Aside.*) But stay, if I introduce myself in this manner, they

will know me to be the King.   Be it so, I will
accost them, nevertheless.

SHAK.   (*Moving a step or two further off* L.) What ! it
still persists in following me.

KING.   (*Advancing hastily, aloud* R.)—
When mighty Puru's offspring sways the earth,
And o'er the wayward holds his threatening rod,
Who dares molest the gentle maids that keep
Their holy vigils here in Kanwa's grove ?
            (*All look at the* KING, *and are embarrassed.*)

ANA.   Kind sir, no outrage has been committed ; only our
dear friend here was teased by the attacks of
a troublesome bee.   (*Points to* SHAKUNTALA.)

KING.   (*Turning to* SHAKUNTALA.)   I trust all is well
with your devotional rites ?   (SHAKUNTALA
stands confused and silent.)

ANA.   All is well, indeed, now that we are honoured by
the reception of a distinguished guest.   Dear
Shakuntalá, go, bring from the hermitage an
offering of flowers, rice, and fruit.   This water
that we have brought will serve to bathe our
guest's feet[7].

KING.   The rites of hospitality are already performed ;
your truly kind words are the best offering I
can receive.

PRIY.   At least be good enough, gentle Sir, to sit down
awhile, and rest yourself on this seat shaded
by the leaves of the Sapta-parna tree.

KING.   You, too, must all be fatigued by your employ-
ment.

ANA.   Dear Shakuntala, there is no impropriety in our
sitting by the side of our guest : come let us
sit down here.   (*All sit down together* C.)

SHAK.   (*Aside.*) How is it that the sight of this man has
made me sensible of emotions inconsistent
with my religious vows ?

KING.   (*Gazing at them all by turns.*)   How charming-
ly your friendship is in keeping with the
equality of your ages and appearance ;

PRIY. (*Aside to* ANASUYA.) Who can this person be, whose lively yet dignified manner, and polite conversation, bespeak him a man of high rank?

ANA. (*Aside.*) I, too, my dear, am very curious to know. I will ask him myself. (*Aloud.*) Your kind words, noble Sir, fill me with confidence, and prompt me to inquire of what regal family our noble guest is the ornament ? what country is now mourning his absence ? and what induced a person so delicately nurtured to expose himself to the fatigue of visiting this grove of penance ?

SHAK. (*Aside.*) Be not troubled, O my heart, Anasúyá is giving utterance to thy thoughts.

KING. (*Aside.*) How now shall I reply ? shall I make myself known, or shall I still disguise my real rank ? I have it ; I will answer her thus. (*Aloud.*) I am the person charged by his majesty, the descendant of Puru, with the administration of justice and religion ; and am come to this sacred grove to satisfy myself that the rites of the hermits are free from obstruction.

ANA. The hermits, then, and all the members of our religious society have now a guardian. (SHAKUNTALA *gazes bashfully at the* KING. *Perceiving the state of her feelings, and of the* KING's. *Aside to* SHAKUNTALA,) Dear Shakuntalá, if father Kanwa were but at home to-day—

SHAK. (*Angrily.*) What if he were ?

PRIY. He would honour this our distinguished guest with an offering of the most precious of his possessions.

SHAK. Go to ! you have some silly idea in your mind. I will not listen to such remarks.

KING. May I be allowed, in my turn, to ask you maidens a few particulars respecting your friend ?

ANA. Your request, Sir, is an honour.

KING.   The sage Kanwa lives in the constant practice of
          austerities.   How then, can this friend of
          yours be called his daughter ?

ANA.   I will explain to you, Sir.   You have heard of an
          illustrious sage of regal caste, Vishvamitra,
          whose family name is Kaushika[8].

KING.   I have.

ANA.   Know that he is the real father of our friend.   The
          venerable Kanwa is only her reputed father.
          He it was who brought her up, when she was
          deserted by her mother.

KING.   (*Aside*) ' Deserted by her mother !' My curiosity
          is excited. (*Aloud*) Pray let me hear the story
          from the beginning.

ANA.   You shall hear it, Sir.   Some time since, this sage
          of regal caste, while performing a most severe
          penance on the banks of the river Godávari,
          excited the jealousy and alarm of the gods ;
          insomuch that they despatched a lovely nymph
          named Menaká to interrupt his devotions.

KING.   The inferior gods, I am aware, are jealous of the
          power which the practice of excessive devo-
          tion confers on mortals.

ANA.   Well then, it happened that Vishvamitra, gazing
          on the bewitching beauty of that nymph at a
          season when, spring being in its glory—(*stops
          short, and appears confused.*)

KING.   The rest may be easily divined.   Shakuntalá,
          then, is the offspring of the nymph ?

ANA.   Just so.

KING.   It is quite intelligible.

       How could a mortal to such charms give birth ?
       The lightning's radiance flashes not from earth.

                    (SHAKUNTALA *remains modestly seated with
                    down cast eyes.*) (*Aside.*) And so my desire
                    has really scope for its indulgence.   Yet I am
                    still distracted by doubts, remembering the

pleasantry of her female companions respecting her wish for a husband. (*aloud.*) I wish to ascertain one point respecting your friend.

Will she be bound by solitary vows
Opposed to love, till her espousals only ?
Or ever dwell with these her cherished fawns,
Whose eyes, in lustre vying with her own,
Return her gaze of sisterly affection ?

PRIY. Hitherto, Sir, she has been engaged in the practice of religious duties, and has lived in subjection to her foster-father ; but it is now his fixed intention to give her away in marriage to a husband worthy of her.

KING. (*Aside.*) His intention may be easily carried into effect.

Be hopeful, O my heart, thy harrowing doubts
Are past and gone ; that which thou didst believe
To be as unapproachable as fire,
Is found a glittering gem that may be touched.

SHAK. (*Pretending anger.*) Anasúyá, I shall leave you.
ANA. Why so ?
SHAK. That I may go and report this impertinent Priyamvadá to the venerable matron Gautamí.
PRIY. (*Holding* SHAKUNTALA *back.*) Dear Shakuntalá, it does not become you to go away in this manner.
SHAK. (*Frowning.*) Why not, pray ?
PRIY. You are under a promise to water two more shrubs for me. When you have paid your debt, you shall go, and not before. (*Forces her to turn back.*)
KING. Spare her this trouble, gentle maiden. The exertion of watering the shrubs has already fatigued her. Suffer me, then, thus to discharge the debt for you. (*Offers a ring to* PRIYAMVADA. *Both the maidens, reading*

the name DUSHYANTA *on the seal, look at each other with surprise.)*

PRIY. (*With a smile.*) Now, Shakuntalá my love, you are at liberty to retire, thanks to the intercession of this noble stranger, or rather of this mighty prince.

SHAK. (*Aside.*) My movements are no longer under my own control. (*Aloud.*) Pray, what authority have you over me, either to send me away or keep me back?

KING. (*Gazing at* SHAKUNTALA.) (*Aside*) Would I could ascertain whether she is affected towards me as I am towards her! At any rate, my hopes are free to indulge themselves.

A VOICE (*within.*) O hermits, be ready to protect the animals belonging to our hermitage. King Dushyanta, amusing himself with hunting, is near at hand.

KING. (*Aside.*) Out upon it! my retinue are looking for me, and are disturbing this holy retreat. Well! there is no help for it; I must go and meet them.

PRIY. Noble Sir, we are terrified by the accidental disturbance caused by the wild elephant. Permit us to return into the cottage.

KING. (*Hastily.*) Go, gentle maidens. It shall be our care that no injury happen to the hermitage. (*All rise up.*)

SHAK. Anasúyá, a pointed blade of Kuhsa-grass 9 has pricked my foot; and my bark-mantle is caught in the branch of a Kuruvaka-bush.10 Be so good as to wait for me until I have disentangled it. (*Exit with her two companions, after making pretexts for delay, that she may steal glances at the* KING L.)

KING. I have no longer any desire to return to the city. I will therefore rejoin my attendants, and make them encamp somewhere in the vicinity

of this sacred grove. In good truth, Shakuntalá has taken such possession of my
thoughts, that I cannot turn myself in any
other direction.

My limbs drawn onward leave my heart behind,
Like silken pennon borne against the wind. (*Exit* R.)

~~~~~~~~~~~~~~~

ACT II.

SCENE.—*A plain on the skirts of the forest.*

Enter the Jester MATHAVYA, *in a melancholy mood* L.

MATH. (*Sighing.*) Heigh-ho ! what an unlucky fellow
I am ! worn to a shadow by my royal friend's
sporting propensities. ' Here's a deer !'
' There goes a boar !' ' Yonder's a tiger !'
This is the only burden of our talk, while in
the heat of the meridian sun we toil on from
jungle to jungle, wandering about in the
paths of the woods, where the trees afford us
no shelter. Are we thirsty ? We have
nothing to drink but the foul water of some
mountain stream, filled with dry leaves which
give it a most pungent flavour. Are we
hungry ? We have nothing to eat but roast
game, which we must swallow down at odd
times, as best we can. Even at night there
is no peace to be had. Sleeping is out of the
question, with joints all strained by dancing
attendance upon my sporting friend ; or if I
do happen to doze, I am awakened at the very
earliest dawn by the horrible din of a lot of
rascally beaters and huntsmen, who must
needs surround the wood before sunrise, and

deafen me with their clatter. Nor are these
my only troubles. Here's a fresh grievance,
like a new boil rising upon an old one ! Yes-
terday, while we were lagging behind, my
royal friend entered yonder hermitage after a
deer ; and there, as ill-luck would have it,
caught sight of a beautiful girl, called Shakuntalá, the hermit's daughter. From that
moment, not another thought about returning
to the city ! and all last night, not a wink of
sleep did he get for thinking of the damsel.
What is to be done ? At any rate I will be
on the watch for him as soon as he has
finished his toilet. (*Walking* C. *and looking
about.*)   Oh ! here he comes, attended by the
Yavana women with bows in their hands, and
wearing garlands of wild flowers. What shall
I do ?   I have it.   I will pretend to stand in
the easiest attitude for resting my bruised and
crippled limbs. (*Stands leaning on a staff* L.)

Enter King DUSHYANTA, *followed by a retinue of*
YAVANA WOMEN R. U. E.

KING.   True, by no easy conquest may I win her,
Yet are my hopes encouraged by her mien.
Love is not yet triumphant ; but, methinks,
The hearts of both are ripe for his delights.

(*Smiling.*)   Ah ! thus does the lover delude
himself ; judging of the state of his loved one's
feelings by his own desires.

MATH.   (*Still in the same attitude.*)   Ah, friend, my
hands cannot move to greet you with the
usual salutation.   I can only just command
my lips to wish your majesty victory.

KING.   Why, what has paralysed your limbs ?

MATH.   You might as well ask me how my eye comes to
water after you have poked your finger into it.

KING.   I don't understand you ; speak more intelligibly.

MATH. Ah, my dear friend, is yonder upright reed trans-
formed into a crooked plant by its own act, or
by the force of the current ?

KING. The current of the river causes it, I suppose.

MATH. Aye ; just as you are the cause of my crippled
limbs.

KING. How so ?

MATH. Here are you living the life of a wild man of the
woods in a savage unfrequented region, while
your state affairs are left to shift for themselves ; and as for poor me, I am no longer
master of my own limbs, but have to follow
you about day after day in your chases after
wild animals, till my bones are all crippled
and out of joint. Do, my dear friend, let me
have one day's rest.

KING. (*Aside.*) This fellow little knows, while he talks
in this manner, that my mind is wholly en-
grossed by recollections of the hermit's
daughter, and quite as disinclined to the chase
as his own.

MATH. (*Looking in the* KING'S *face,*) I may as well
speak to the winds, for any attention you pay
to my requests. I suppose you have something on your mind, and are talking it over
to yourself.

KING. (*Smiling.*) I was only thinking that I ought
not to disregard a friend's request.

MATH. Then may the King live for ever! (*Moves off* R.)

KING. Stay a moment, my dear friend I have something
else to say to you.

MATH. Say on, then.

KING. When you have rested, you must assist me in
another business, which will give you no
fatigue.

MATH. In eating something nice, I hope.

KING. You shall know at some future time.

MATH. No time better than the present.

KING. What ho ! there,

WARD. What are your Majesty's commands ?

KING. O Raivatika ! bid the General of the forces attend.

WARD. I will, Sire, (*Exit* L.)

Re-enter WARDER *with the* GENERAL L.

WARD. Come forward, General ; his Majesty is looking
       towards you, and has some order to give you.

GEN. (*Approaching the* KING.) Victory to the King !
       We• have tracked the wild beasts to their
       lairs in the forest. Why delay, when every-
       thing is ready ?

KING. My frind Mathavya here has been disparaging
       the chase, till he has taken away all my relish
       for it.

GEN. (*Aside to* MATHAVYA.) Persevere in your oppo-
       sition, my good fellow : I will sound the
       King's real feelings, and humour him accord-
       ingly. (*Aloud.*) The blockhead talks non-
       sense, and your Majesty, in your own person
       furnishes the best poof of it. Observe, sire,
       the advantage and pleasure the huuter derives
       from the chase.

              Oh ! 'tis conceit
In moralists to call the chase a vice;
What recreation can compare with this?

MATH. (*Angrily.*) Away! tempter, away! The King
       has recovered his senses, and is himself again.
       As for you, you may, if you choose, wander
       about from forest to forest, till some old bear
       seizes you by the nose, and makes a mouthful
       of you.

KING. My good General, as we are just now in the neigh-
       bourhood of a consecrated grove, your panegy-
       ric upon hunting is somewhat ill-timed, and
       I cannot assent to all you have said.

GEN. So please your Majesty, it shall be as you desire.

KING.   Recal, then, the beaters who were sent in advance
         to surround the forest. My troops must not
         be allowed to disturb this sacred retreat, and
         irritate its pious inhabitants.

GEN.   Your Majesty's commands shall be obeyed.

MATH.   Off with you, you son of a slave! Your nonsense
         won't go down here, my fine fellow. (*Exit*
         GENERAL R.)

KING.   (*Looking at his attendants.*) Here, women,
         take my hunting-dress ; and you, Raivatika,
         keep guard carefully outside.

ATTEND. We will, sire. (*Exeunt* L.)

MATH.   Now that you have got rid of these plagues, who
         have been buzzing about us like so many flies,
         sit down, do, on that stone slab, with the
         shade of the tree as your canopy, and I will
         seat myself by you quite comfortably.

KING.   Go you, and sit down first.

MATH.   Come along, then. (*Both walk on a little way*, R.
         and seat themselves R.)

KING.   Mathavya, it may be said of you that you have
         never beheld anything worth seeing : for your
         eyes have not yet looked upon the loveliest
         object in creation.

MATH.   How can you say so, when I see your Majesty
         before me at this moment ?

KING.   It is very natural that every one should consider
         his own friend perfect ; but I was alluding to
         Shakuntala, the brightest ornament of these
         hallowed groves.

MATH.   (*Aside.*) I understand well enough, but I am
         not going to humour him. (*Aloud.*) If, as
         you intimate, she is a hermit's daughter,
         you cannot lawfully ask her in marriage.
         You may as well, then, dismiss her from your
         mind, for any good the mere sight of her
         can do.

KING.   Think you that a descendant of the mighty Puru
         could fix his affections on an unlawful object ?

MATH. (*Smiling.*) This passion of yours for a rustic maiden, when you have so many gems of women at home in your palace, seems to me very like the fancy of a man who is tired of sweet dates, and longs for sour tamarinds as a variety.

KING. You have not seen her, or you would not talk in this fashion.

MATH. I can quite understand; it must require something surpassingly attractive to excite the admiration of such a great man as you.

KING. I will describe her, my dear friend, in a few words :—

Man's all-wise Maker wishing to create
A faultless form, whose matchless symmetry
Should far transcend Creation's choicest works,
Did call together by his mighty will,
And garner up in his eternal mind,
A bright assemblage of all lovely things ;
And then, as in a picture, fashion them
Into one perfect and ideal form.
Such the divine, the wondrous prototype,
Whence her fair shape was moulded into being.

MATH. If that's the case, she must indeed throw all other beauties into the shade.

KING. To my mind she really does :

This peerless maid is like a fragrant flower,
Whose perfumed breath has never been diffused ;
A tender bud, that no profaning hand
Has dared to sever from its parent stalk ;
A gem of priceless water, just released,
Pure and unblemished, from its glittering bed.
Or may the maiden haply be compared
To sweetest honey, that no mortal lip
Has sipped ; or, rather to the mellowed fruit
Of virtuous actions in some former birth,[2]
Now brought to full perfection.   Lives the man
Whom bounteous heaven has destined to espouse her ?

MATH.   Make haste, then, to her aid ; you have no time to lose, if you don't wish this fruit of all the virtues to drop into the mouth of some greasy-headed rustic of devout habits.

KING.   The lady is not her own mistress, and her foster-father is not at home.

MATH.   Well, but tell me, did she look at all kindly upon you ?

KING.   Maidens brought up in a hermitage are naturally shy and reserved ; but for all that,

She did look towards me, though she quick withdrew
Her stealthy glances when she met my gaze ;
She smiled upon me sweetly, but disguised
With maiden grace the secret of her smiles.

MATH.   Why, of course, my dear friend, you never could seriously expect that at the very first sight she would fall over head and ears in love with you, and without more ado come and sit in your lap.

KING.   When we parted from each other, she betrayed her liking for me by clearer indications, but still with the utmost modesty.

MATH.   I trust you have laid in a good stock of provisions, for I see you intend making this conse-crated grove your game-preserve, and will be roaming here in quest of sport for some time to come.

KING.   You must know, my good fellow, that I have been recognised by some of the inmates of the hermitage. Now I want the assistance of your fertile invention, in devising some excuse for going there again.

MATH.   There is but one expedient that I can suggest, You are the King, are you not ?

KING.   What then ?

MATH.   Say you have come for the sixth part of their grain, which they owe you for tribute.

KING.   No, no, foolish man ; these hermits pay me a very
different kind of tribute, which I value more
than heaps of gold or jewels ; observe,
The tribute which my other subjects bring
Must moulder into dust, but holy men
Present me with a portion of the fruits
Of penitential services and prayers—
A precious and imperishable gift.

A VOICE (*Within*).   We are fortunate ; here is the object
of our search.

KING.   (*Listening.*)   Surely those must be the voices of
hermits, to judge by their deep tones.

ENTER WARDER R.

WAR.   Victory to the King ! two young hermits are in
waiting outside, and solicit an audience of
your Majesty.

KING.   Introduce them immediately.

WAR.   I will, my liege.   (*Exit* R.)

Re-enter WARDER *with* TWO YOUNG HERMITS R.
Looking at the KING.

WAR.   This way, Sirs, this way.

1ST HER.   How majestic is his mien, and yet what confidence it inspires !   But this might be ex-
pected in a king, whose character and habits
have earned for him a title only one degree
removed from that of a Saint.3

2ND HER.   Bear in mind, Gautama, that this is the great
Dushyanta, the friend of Indra.

1ST HER.   (*Approaching.*)   Victory to the King !

KING.   (*Rising from his seat.*)   Hail to you both !

2ND HER.   (*He offers fruits.*)   Heaven bless your
majesty !

KING.   (*Respectfully receiving the offering.*)   Tell me,
I pray you, the object of your visit.

1ST HER.   The inhabitants of the hermitage having heard
of your Majesty's sojourn in our neighbourhood, make this humble petition.

KING.   What are their commands ?

2ND HER. In the absence of our Superior, the great Sage
         Kanwa, evil demons are disturbing our sacri-
         ficial rites.4   Deign, therefore, accompanied
         by your charioteer, to take up your abode in
         our hermitage for a few days.

KING.   I am honoured by your invitation.

MATH.   (*Aside.*) Most opportune and convenient, cer-
         tainly !

KING.   (*Smiling.*) Ho ! there, Raivatika ! Tell the
         charioteer from me to bring round the chariot
         with my bow.

WAR.   I will, Sire. (*Exit* L.)

KING.   (*Bowing to the* HERMITS.) Go first, reverend
         Sirs, I will follow you immediately.

1ST HER. May victory attend you ! (*Exeunt both* R.)

KING.   My dear Máthavya, are you not full of longing to
         see Shakuntalá ?

MATH.   To tell you the truth, though I was just now
         brim-full of desire to see her, I have not a
         drop left since this piece of news about the
         demons.

KING.   Never fear ; you shall keep close to me for pro-
         tection.

MATH.   Well, you must be my guardian-angel, and act
         the part of a very Vishnu5 to me.

             Re-enter WARDER L.

WAR.   Sire, the chariot is ready, and only waits to
         conduct you to victory. But here is a mes-
         senger named Karabhaka, just arrived from
         your capital, with a message from the Queen,
         your mother.

KING.   (*Respectfully.*) How say you ? a messenger from
         the venerable Queen ?

WAR.   Even so.

KING.   Introduce him at once.

WAR.   I will, Sire. (*Exit* L.)

      Re-enter WARDER *with* KARABHAKA L,

WAR.   Behold the King ! Approach.

KAR. (*Approaching.*) Victory to the King ! The Queen-mother bids me say that in four days from the present time she intends celebrating a solemn ceremony for the advancement and preservation of her son. She expects that your Majesty will honour her with your presence on that occasion.

KING. This places me in a dilemma. Here, on the one hand, is the commission of these holy men to be executed ; and, on the other, the command of my revered parent to be obeyed. Both duties are too sacred to be neglected. What is to be done ?

MATH. You will have to take up an intermediate position between the two, like King Trishanku, who was suspended between heaven and earth, because the sage Vishvamitra commanded him to mount up to heaven, and the gods ordered him down again.

KING. I am certainly very much perplexed. (*Reflecting.*) Friend Mathavya, as you were my playfellow in childhood, the Queen has always received you like a second son ; go you, then, back to her and tell her of my solemn engagement to assist these holy men. You can supply my place in the ceremony, and act the part of a son to the Queen.

MATH. With the greatest pleasure in the world ; but don't suppose that I am really coward enough to have the slightest fear of those trumpery demons.

KING. (*Smiling.*) Oh ! of course not ; a great Bráhman like you could not possibly give way to such weakness.

MATH. You must let me travel in a manner suitable to the King's younger brother.

KING. Yes, I shall send my retinue with you, that there

may be no further disturbance in this sacred forest.

MATH. (*With a strut.*) Already I feel quite like a young prince.

KING. (*Aside.*) This is a giddy fellow, and in all probability he will let out the truth about my present pursuit to the women of the palace. What is to be done ? I must say something to deceive him. (*Aloud to* MATHAVYA, *taking him by the hand.*) Dear friend, I am going to the hermitage, wholly and solely out of respect for its pious inhabitants, and not because I have really any liking for Shakuntalá, the hermit's daughter. Observe,

What suitable communion could there be
Between a monarch and a rustic girl ?
I did but feign an idle passion, friend,
Take not in earnest what was said in jest.

MATH. Don't distress yourself ; I quite understand.

(*Exeunt* L.)

ACT III.

SCENE.—*The Sacred Grove.*

Enter KING DUSHYANTA, L. *with the air of one in love.*

KING. Adorable god of love ! hast thou no pity for me ? (*In a tone of anguish.*) How can thy arrows be so sharp when they are pointed with flowers ? (*Glancing at the sun.*) In all probability, as the sun's heat is now at its height, Shakuntalá is passing her time under the shade of the bowers on the banks of the Málini,

attended by her maidens. I will go and look
for her there. (*Walking and looking about.*)
I suspect the fair one has but just passed by
this avenue of young trees. She must be
somewhere in the neighbourhood of this arbour
of overhanging creepers, enclosed by plantations of cane. (*Looking down.*) I will peep
through those branches. (*Walking and
looking. With transport.*) Ah! now my
eyes are gratified by an entrancing sight.
Yonder is the beloved of my heart reclining
on a rock strewn with flowers, and attended by
her two friends. How fortunate! Concealed
behind the leaves, I will listen to their conversation, without raising their suspicions.
(*Stands concealed* L, *and gazes at them.*)

SHAKUNTALA, *and her two attendants, holding fans
in their hands, are discovered on a rock
strewn with flowers,* C.

PRIY. (*Fanning her. In a tone of affection.*) Dearest
Shakuntalá, is the breeze raised by these broad
lotus-leaves refreshing to you?

SHAK. Dear friends, why should you trouble yourselves
to fan me? (PRIYAMVADA *and* ANASUYA
look sorrowfully at one another.)

KING. Shakuntalá seems indeed to be seriously ill.
(*Thoughtfully.*) Can it be the intensity of
the heat that has affected her? or does
my heart suggest the true cause of her mala-
dy? (*Gazing at her passionately.*) Why
should I doubt it?

PRIY. (*Aside to* ANASUYA.) I have observed Anasúyá,
that Shakuntalá has been indisposed ever since
her first interview with King Dushyanta.
Depend upon it, her ailment is to be traced to
this source.

ANA. The same suspicion, dear, has crossed my mind.
But I will at once ask her and ascertain the

truth. (*Aloud.*) Dear Shakuntalá, I am about to put a question to you. Your indisposition is really very serious.

SHAK. (*Half-rising from her couch.*) What were you going to ask ?

ANA. We know very little about love-matters, dear Shakuntalá ; but for all that, I cannot help suspecting your present state to be something similar to that of the lovers we have read about in romances. Tell us frankly what is the cause of your disorder. It is useless to apply a remedy, until the disease be understood.

KING. Anasúyá bears me out in my suspicion.

SHAK. (*Aside.*) I am, indeed, deeply in love ; but cannot rashly disclose my passion to these young girls. (*Aloud*) Know then, dear friends that from the first moment the illustrious Prince, who is the guardian of our sacred grove, presented himself to my sight—(*Stops short, and appears confused.*)

ANA. Say on, dear Shakuntalá, say on.

SHAK. Ever since that happy moment, my heart's affections have been fixed upon him, and my energies of mind and body have all deserted me, as you see.

KING. (*With rapture.*) Her own lips have uttered the words I most longed to hear.

SHAK. You must consent, then, dear friends, to contrive some means by which I may find favour with the King, or you will have ere long to assist at my funeral.

KING. Enough ! These words remove all my doubts.

PRIY. (*Aside to* ANASUYA.) She is far gone in love dear Anasúyá, and no time ought to be lost. Since she has fixed her affections on a monarch, who is the ornament of Puru's line, we need not hesitate for a moment to express our approval.

ANA. I quite agree with you.

PRIY. (*Aloud.*) We wish you joy, dear Shakuntalá. Your affections are fixed on an object in every respect worthy of you. The noblest river will unite itself to the ocean, and the lovely Mádhaví-creeper clings naturally to the Mango, the only tree capable of supporting it.

ANA. By what stratagem can we best secure to our friend the accomplishment of her heart's desire both speedily and secretly ?

PRIY. The latter point is all we have to think about. As to ' speedily,' I look upon the whole affair as already settled.

ANA. How so ?

PRIY. Did you not observe how the King betrayed his liking by the tender manner in which he gazed upon her, and how thin he has become the last few days, as if he had been lying awake thinking of her ?

KING. (*Looking at himself.*) Quite true ! I certainly am becoming thin from want of sleep.

PRIY. (*Thoughtfully.*) An idea strikes me, Anasúyá. Let Shakuntalá write a love-letter ; I will conceal it in a flower, and contrive to drop it in the King's path. He will surely mistake it for the remains of some sacred offering, and will, in all probability, pick it up.

ANA. A very ingenious device ! It has my entire approval ; but what says Shakuntalá ?

SHAK. I must consider before I can consent to it.

PRIY. Could you not, dear Shakuntalá, think of some pretty composition in verse, containing a delicate declaration of your love ?

SHAK. Well, I will do my best ; but my heart trembles when I think of the chances of a refusal.

KING. (*Aside. With rapture.*)
Too timid maid, here stands the man from whom
Thou fearest a repulse ; supremely blessed
To call thee all his own. Well might he doubt
His title to thy love ; but how could'st thou
Believe thy beauty powerless to subdue him ?

PRIY. You undervalue your own merits, dear Shakuntalá. What man in his senses would intercept
with the skirt of his robe the bright rays of
the autumnal moon, which alone can allay
the fever of his body ?

SHAK. (*Smiling.*) Then it seems I must do as I am
bid. (*Sits down and appears to be thinking.*)

KING. How charming she looks ! My very eyes forget
to wink, jealous of losing even for an instant
a sight so enchanting.

SHAK. Dear girls, I have thought of a verse, but I have
no writing-materials at hand.

PRIY. Write the letters with your nail on this lotus-leaf,
which is smooth as a parrot's breast.

SHAK. (*After writing the verse.*) Listen, dear friends,
and tell me whether the ideas are appropriately expressed.

ANA. We are all attention.

SHAK. (*Sings.*)

" I know not the secret thy bosom conceals,
    Thy form is not near me to gladden my sight ;
But sad is the tale that my fever reveals,
    Of the love that consumes me by day and by night."

KING. (*Advancing hastily towards her.*)
Nay, Love does but warm thee, fair maiden,—thy frame
    Only droops like the bud in the glare of the noon ;
But me he consumes with a pitiless flame,
    As the beams of the day-star destroy the pale moon.

PRIY. (*Looking at him joyfully, and rising to salute
him.*) Welcome, the desire of our hearts,
that so speedily presents itself ! (SHAKUN-
TALA *makes an effort to rise.*)

KING.　Nay, trouble not thyself, dear maiden,
　　　Move not to do me homage ; let thy limbs
　　　Still softly rest upon their flowery couch,
　　　And gather fragrance from the lotus-stalks
　　　Bruised by the fevered contact of thy frame.

ANA.　Deign, gentle Sir, to seat yourself on the rock on
　　　which our friend is reposing. (*The* KING
　　　sits down. SHAKUNTALA *is confused.*)

PRIY.　Any one may see at a glance that you are deeply
　　　attached to each other. But the affection I
　　　have for my friend prompts me to say some-
　　　thing of which you hardly require to be in-
　　　formed.

KING.　Do not hesitate to speak out, my good girl. If
　　　you omit to say what is in your mind, you
　　　may be sorry for it afterwards.

PRIY.　Is it not your special office as a King to remove
　　　the suffering of your subjects, who are in
　　　trouble ?

KING.　Such is my duty, most assuredly.

PRIY.　Know, then that our dear friend has been brought
　　　to her present state of suffering entirely
　　　through love for you. Her life is in your
　　　hands ; take pity on her and restore her to
　　　health.

KING.　Excellent maiden, our attachment is mutual. It
　　　is I who am the most honoured by it.

SHAK.　(*Looking at* PRIYAMVADA.) What do you mean
　　　by detaining the King, who must be anxious
　　　to return to his royal consorts after so long a
　　　separation ?

KING.　Sweet maiden, banish from thy mind the thought
　　　That I could love another. Thou dost reign
　　　Supreme, without a rival, in my heart,
　　　And I am thine alone : disown me not,
　　　Else must I die a second deadlier death,—
　　　Killed by thy words, as erst by Káma's[1] shafts.

ANA   Kind sir, we have heard it said that kings have
        many favourite consorts. You must not,
        then, by your behaviour towards our dear
        friend, give her relations cause to sorrow for
        her.

KING.   Listen, gentle maiden, while in a few words I
        quiet your anxiety.
   Though many beauteous forms my palace grace,
   Henceforth two things alone will I esteem
   The glory of my royal dynasty :—
   My sea-girt realm, and this most lovely maid.

ANA.   We are satisfied by your assurances.

PRIY.   (*Glancing on one side.*)   See, Anasúyá there is
        our favourite little fawn running about in
        great distress, and turning its eyes in every
        direction as if looking for its mother ; come,
        let us help the little thing to find her. (*Both
        move away* R.)

SHAK.   Dear friends, dear friends, leave me not alone and
        unprotected. Why need you both go ?

PRIY.   Unprotected ! when the Protector of the world is
        at your side. (*Exeunt* R.)

SHAK.   What ! have they both really left me ?

KING.   Distress not thyself, sweet maiden. Thy adorer
        is at hand to wait upon thee.

SHAK.   Nay, touch me not. I will not incur the censure
        of those whom I am bound to respect. (*Rises
        and attempts to go* R.)

KING.   Fair one, the heat of noon has not yet subsided,
        and thy body is still feeble. (*Forces her to
        turn back.*)

SHAK.   Infringe not the rules of decorum, mighty des-
        cendant of Puru. Remember, though I love
        you, I have no power to dispose of myself.

KING.   Why this fear of offending your relations, timid
        maid ? When your venerable foster-father
        hears of it, he will not find fault with you.

He knows that the law permits us to be united without consulting him.

SHAK. Leave me, leave me ; I must take counsel with my female friends.

KING. I will leave thee when—

SHAK. When ?

KING. When I have gently stolen from thy lips
Their yet untasted nectar, to allay
The raging of my thirst, e'en as the bee
Sips the fresh honey from the opening bud. (*Attempts to raise her face.* SHAKUNTALA *tries to prevent him.*)

A VOICE (*Within*). The loving birds, doomed by fate to nightly separation,[2] must bid farewell to each other, for evening is at hand.

SHAK. (*In confusion.*) Great Prince, I hear the voice of the matron Gautamí. She is coming this way, to inquire after my health. Let me go. (*Exit* R.)

KING. (*Returning to his former seat in the arbour. Sighing.*) Alas ! how many are the obstacles to the accomplishment of our wishes ! Whither now shall I betake myself ? I will tarry for a brief space in this bower of creepers, so endeared to me by the presence of my beloved Shakuntalá. (*Looking round.*)

A VOICE IN THE AIR. (*Thunder &c.*) Great King,

Scarce is our evening sacrifice begun,
When evil demons, lurid as the clouds
That gather round the dying orb of day,
Cluster in hideous troops, obscene and dread,
About our altars, casting far and near
Terrific shadows, while the sacred fire
Sheds a pale lustre o'er their ghostly shapes.

KING. I come to the rescue, I come. (*Exit* R.)

ACT IV.

Scene.— *The Hermitage.*

Enter Priyamvada *and* Anasuya c. *joyfully.*

Pri.—Quick ! quick ! Anasúyá ! come and assist in the
    joyful preparations for Shakuntalá's departure
    to her husband's palace.

Ana. My dear girl, what can you mean ?

Priy. Listen, now, and I will tell you all about it. I
    went just now to Shakuntalá, to inquire whe-
    ther she had slept comfortably——

Ana. Well, well ; go on.

Priy. She was sitting with her face bowed down to the
    very ground with shame, when father Kanwa
    entered and, embracing her, of his own ac-
    cord offered her his congratulations. ' I give
    thee joy, my child,' he said, ' we have had an
    auspicious omen. The priest who offered the
    oblation dropped it into the very centre of the
    sacred fire,[1] though thick smoke obstructed
    his vision. Henceforth thou wilt cease to be
    an object of compassion. This very day I
    purpose sending thee, under the charge of
    certain trusty hermits, to the King's palace ;
    and shall deliver thee into the hands of thy
    husband, as I would commit knowledge to the
    keeping of a wise and faithful student.

Ana. Who, then informed the holy Father of what
    passed in his absence ?

Priy. As he was entering the sanctuary of the conse-
    crated fire, an invisible being chanted a verse
    in celestial strains.

Ana. (*With astonishment.*) Indeed ! pray repeat it.

Priy. (*Repeating the verse*),

" Glows in thy daughter King Dushyanta's glory,
  As in the sacred tree the mystic fire.[2]
Let worlds rejoice to hear the welcome story ;
And may the son immortalize the sire."

ANA.   (*Embracing* PRIYAMVADA.)   Oh, my dear Priy-
        amvadá, what delightful news !   I am pleased
        beyond measure ; yet when I think that we
        are to lose our dear Shakuntalá this very day,
        a feeling of melancholy mingles with my joy.

PRIY.   We shall find means of consoling ourselves after
        her departure.   Let the dear creature only be
        made happy, at any cost.

ANA.   Yes, yes, Priyamvadá, it shall be so ; and now to
        prepare our bridal array.   I have always
        looked forward to this occasion, and some
        time since, I deposited a beautiful garland of
        Keshara flowers in a cocoa-nut box, and sus-
        pended it on a bough of yonder mango-tree.
        Be good enough to stretch out your hand
        and take it down, while I compound unguents
        and perfumes with this consecrated paste and
        these blades of sacred grass.

PRIY.   Very well. (*Exit* ANASUYA. L. PRIYAMVADA
        takes down the flowers.)

A VOICE. (*Within.*) Gautamí, bid Shárngarava and the
        others hold themselves in readiness to escort
        Shakuntalá.

PRIY.   (*Listening.*) Quick, quick, Anasúya ! They are
        calling the hermits who are to go with Sha-
        kuntalá to Hastinapur.[3]

Re-enter ANASUYA L. *with the perfumed unguents in
        her hand.*

ANA.   Come along then, Priyamvadá ; I am ready to go
        with you. (*They walk away* R.)

PRIY.   (*Looking.*) See ! there sits Shakuntalá, her
        locks arranged even at this early hour of the
        morning. The holy women of the hermitage
        are congratulating her, and invoking blessings

on her head, while they present her with
wedding-gifts and offerings of consecrated
wild-rice. Let us join them. Let us join
them. (*Exit* R.)

SCENE II.—*A room in the Hermitage*

SHAKUNTALA *is seen seated* C., *with* GOUTAMI *and other
women surrounding and decorating her, preparatory
to her dispatch to her husband's palace*

PRIY. (*Approaching.*) Dear Shakuntalá, we are come
to assist you at your toilet, and may a blessing attend it !

SHAK. Welcome, dear friends, welcome. Sit down here.

ANA. (*Taking the baskets containing the bridal decorations, and sitting down.*) Now, then,
dearest, prepare to let us dress you. We
must first rub your limbs with these perfumed
unguents. (*They rub* SHAKUNTALA'S *hands
with unguents.*)

SHAK. I ought indeed to be grateful for your kind
offices, now that I am so soon to be deprived
of them. Dear, dear friends, perhaps I shall
never be dressed by you again. (*Bursts into
tears.*)

ANA. Weep not, dearest ; tears are out of season on
such a happy occasion. (*They wipe away
her tears and begin to dress her.*)

PRIY. Alas ! these simple flowers and rude ornaments
which our hermitage offers in abundance, do
not set off your beauty as it deserves.

Enter TWO YOUNG HERMITS R. *bearing costly presents.*

BOTH HER. Here are ornaments suitable for a queen.
(*The women look at them in astonishment.*)

GAUT. Why, Nárada, my son, whence came these ?

1ST HER. You owe them to the devotion of Father
Kanwa.

GAUT. Did he create them by the power of his own
mind ?

2ND HER.   Certainly not ; but you shall hear. The
venerable sage ordered us to collect flowers
for Shakuntala from the forest-trees ; and we
went to the wood for that purpose, when

> Straightway depending from a neighbouring tree
> Appeared a robe of linen tissue, pure
> And spotless as a moonbeam—mystic pledge
> Of bridal happiness ; another tree   -
> Distilled a roseate dye wherewith to stain
> The lady's feet ; 4 and other branches near
> Glistened with rare and costly ornaments.
> While, 'midst the leaves, the hands of forest-nymphs,
> Vying in beauty with the opening buds,
> Presented us with sylvan offerings.

PRIY.   (*Looking at* SHAKUNTALA.)   The wood-nymphs
have done you honour, indeed. This favour
doubtless signifies that you are soon to be
received as a happy wife into your husband's
house, and are from this forward to become
the partner of his royal fortunes. (SHAKUN-
TALA *appears confused.*)

1ST HER.   Come, Gautama ; Father Kanwa has finished
his ablutions. Let us go and inform him of
the favour we have received from the deities
who preside over our trees.

2ND HER.   By all means. (*Exeunt both the* HERMITS R.)

PRIY.   Alas ! what are we to do? We are unused to
such splendid decorations, and are at a loss
how to arrange them. Our knowledge of
painting must be our guide. We will dispose
the ornaments as we have seen them in
pictures. Let us go in.

SHAK.   Whatever pleases you, dear girls, will please me.
I have perfect confidence in your taste.
(*Exeunt* OMNES R.)   3

Enter KANWA, L. *having just finished his ablutions.*

KAN. This day my loved one leaves me, and my heart
Is heavy with its grief : the streams of sorrow
Choked at the source, repress my faltering voice.
I have no words to speak ; mine eyes are dimmed
By the dark shadows of the thoughts that rise
Within my soul. If such the force of grief
In an old hermit parted from his nursling,
What anguish must the stricken parent feel—
Bereft for ever of an only daughter. (*Retires* R.
up the stage.)

Re-enter SHAKUNTALA, *gaily dressed and decorated
preparatory to her going to her husband's palace,
accompanied by* ANASUYA, PRIYAMVADA, GAUTAMI *and
other women.*

ANA. Now, dearest Shakuntalá, we have finished decorating you. You have only to put on the
two linen mantles. (SHAKUNTALA *rises and
puts them on.*)

GAUT. Daughter, see, here comes thy foster-father ; he
is eager to fold thee in his arms ; his eyes
swim with tears of joy. Hasten to do him
reverence.

KANVA APPROACHES.

SHAK. (*Reverently.*) My father, I salute you.

KAN. My daughter,
May'st thou be highly honoured by thy lord,
Even as Yayáti Sarmishthá adored ! 5
And, as she bore him Puru, so may'st thou
Bring forth a son to whom the world shall bow !

GAUT. Most venerable father, she accepts your benediction as if she already possessed the boon it
confers.

KAN. Now come this way, my child, and walk reverently round these sacrificial fires. (*They all
walk round the holy fire throwing wild rice
consecrated paste, and clarified butter into it*

KAN.   (*Repeats a prayer in the metre of the Rig-veda.*)

Holy flames, that gleam around
Every altar's hallowed ground ;
Holy flames, whose frequent food
Is the consecrated wood,
And for whose encircling bed,
Sacred Kusha-grass is spread ; 6
Holy flames, that waft to heaven
Sweet oblations daily given,
Mortal guilt to purge away ;—
Hear, oh hear me, when I pray—
Purify my child this day !

      Now then, my daughter, set out on thy
journey. (*Looking on one side.*) Where are
thy attendants, Shárngarava and the others ?

Enter an assemblage of HERMITS *consisting of*
SHARANGRAVA, SHARADWAT *and the rest* R.

YOUNG HER.   Here we are, most venerable father.

KAN.   Lead the way for thy sister.

SHARN.   Come, Shakuntalá, let us proceed. (*All move
away* L.)

SHAK.   (*Bowing respectfully and walking on. Aside
to her friend.*) Eager as I am, dear Priyamvadá, to see my husband once more, yet my
feet refuse to move, now that I am quitting
for ever the home of my girlhood.

PRIY.   You are not the only one, dearest, to feel the
bitterness of parting. As the time of separation approaches, the whole grove seems to
share your anguish.

KAN.   Proceed on thy journey, my child. For shame,
Anasúyá! dry your tears. Is this the way to
cheer your friend at a time when she needs
your support and consolation ? (*All move
on* L.)

Weep not, my daughter, check the gathering tear
That lurks beneath thine eyelid, ere it flow
And weaken thy resolve ; be firm and true—
True to thyself and me ; the path of life
Will lead o'er hill and plain, o'er rough and smooth
And all must feel the steepness of the way ;
Though rugged be thy course, press boldly on.

SHARN. Venerable sire ! the sacred precept is—'Accompany thy friend as far as the margin of the first stream.' Here then, we are arrived at the border of a lake. It is time for you to give us your final instructions and return.

KAN. (Aside.) I must think of some appropriate message to send to his majesty King Dushyanta. (Reflecting.) This is it—

Most puissant prince ! we here present before thee
One thou art bound to cherish and receive
As thine own wife ; yea, even to enthrone
As thine own queen—worthy of equal love
With thine imperial consorts. So much, Sire,
We claim of thee as justice due to us,
In virtue of our holy character—
In virtue of thine honourable rank—
In virtue of the pure spontaneous love
That secretly grew up 'twixt thee and her,
Without consent or privity of us.
We ask no more—the rest we freely leave
To thy just feeling and to destiny.

SHARN. A most suitable message. I will take care to deliver it correctly.

KAN. And now, my child, a few words of advice for thee. We hermits, though we live secluded from the world, are not ignorant of worldly matters. Listen, then, my daughter. When thou reachest thy husband's palace, and art admitted into his family,

Honour thy betters ; ever be respectful
To those above thee ; and, should others share

Thy husband's love, ne'er yield thyself a prey
To jealousy ; but ever be a friend,
A loving friend, to those who rival thee
In his affections. Should thy wedded lord
Treat thee with harshness, thou must never be
Harsh in return, but patient and submissive.
Be to thy menials courteous, and to all
Placed under thee, considerate and kind :
Be never self-indulgent, but avoid
Excess in pleasure ; and, when fortune smiles,
Be not puffed up. Thus to thy husband's house
Wilt thou a blessing prove, and not a curse.

> Come, my beloved child, one parting embrace
> for me and for thy companions, and then we
> leave thee.

SHAK. My father, must Priyamvadá and Anasúyá really
return with you ? They are very dear to me.

KAN. Yes, my child ; they, too, in good time, will be
given in marriage to suitable husbands. It
would not be proper for them to accompany
thee to such a public place. But Gautamí
shall be thy companion.

SHAK. (*Embracing him.*) Removed from thy bosom,
my beloved father, like a young tendril of the
sandal-tree torn from its home in the western
mountains,7 how shall I be able to support
life in a foreign soil ?

KAN. Daughter, thy fears are groundless :

Soon shall thy lord prefer thee to the rank
Of his own consort ; and unnumbered cares
Befitting his imperial dignity
Shall constantly engross thee. Then the bliss
Of bearing him a son—a noble boy,
Bright as the day-star, shall transport thy soul
With new delights, and little shalt thou reck
Of the light sorrow that afflicts thee now

At parting from thy father and thy friends.

> (SHAKUNTALA *throws herself at her foster-father's feet.*)   Blessings on thee, my child ! May all my hopes of thee be realized !

SHAK.   (*Approaching her friends.*)   Come, my two loved companions, embrace me both of you together.

PRIY.   (*Embracing her.*)   Dear Shakuntalá remember, if the King should by any chance be slow in recognizing you, you have only to show him this ring, on which his own name is engraved.

SHAK.   The bare thought of it puts me in a tremor.

ANA.   There is no real cause for fear, dearest.   Excessive affection is too apt to suspect evil where none exists.

SHARN.   Come, lady, we must hasten on.   The sun is rising in the heavens.

SHAK.   (*Looking towards the hermitage.*)   Dear father, when shall I ever see this hallowed grove again ?

KAŚ.   I will tell thee ; listen.

When thou hast passed a long and blissful life
As King Dushyanta's queen, and jointly shared
With all the earth his ever-watchful care ;
And hast beheld thine own heroic son,
Matchless in arms, united to a spouse
In happy wedlock ; when his aged sire,
Thy faithful husband, hath to him resigned
The helm of state ; then, weary of the world
Together with Dushyanta thou shalt seek
The calm seclusion of thy former home : 8
There amid holy scenes to be at peace,
Till thy pure spirit gain its last release.

> Go, my daughter, and may thy journey be prosperous. (*Exit* SHAKUNTALA *with her escort* R.)

PRIY. Holy father, the sacred grove will be a desert
without Shakuntalá. How can we ever re-
turn to it ?   .

KAN. It is natural enough that your affection should
make you view it in this light. (*Walking
pensively on.*) As for me, I am quite sur-
prised at myself. Now that I have fairly
dismissed her to her husband's house, my
mind is easy : for indeed,

A daughter is a loan—a precious jewel
Lent to a parent till her husband claim her.
And now that to her rightful lord and master
I have delivered her, my burdened soul
Is lightened, and I seem to breathe more freely.

(Exeunt L.)

ACT V.

SCENE.—*A Room in the Palace.*

Enter the CHAMBERLAIN.[1] R.

CHAM. Alas ! to what an advanced period of life have
I attained !

Even this wand betrays the lapse of years ;
In youthful days 'twas but a useless badge
And symbol of my office ; now it serves
As a support to prop my tottering steps.

Ah me ! I feel very unwilling to announce to
the King that a deputation of young hermits
from the sage Kanwa has arrived, and craves
an immediate audience. Certainly, his majesty
ought not to neglect a matter of sacred duty,
yet I hardly like to trouble him when he has
just risen from the judgment-seat. Well

well ; a monarch's business is to sustain the world, and he must not expect much repose ; I will therefore deliver my message. (*Walking on* L. *and looking about.*) Ah ! here comes the King :—

Enter KING DUSHYANTA R., *accompanied by his* WARDER.

CHAM. (*Approaching.*) Victory to the King ! So please your majesty, some hermits who live in a forest near the Snowy Mountains have arrived here, bringing certain women with them. They have a message to deliver from the sage Kanwa, and desire an audience. I await your majesty's commands.

KING. (*Respectfully.*) A message from the sage Kanwa, did you say ?

CHAM. Even so, my liege.

KING. Tell my domestic priest Somaráta to receive the hermits with due honour, according to the prescribed form. He may then himself introduce them into my presence. I will await them in a place suitable for the reception of such holy guests.

CHAM. Your majesty's commands shall be obeyed. (*Exit* R.)

KING. (*Rising and addressing the* WARDER.) Raivatika, lead the way to the chamber of the consecrated fire.[2]

WAR. This way, sire.

KING. (*Walking on, with the air of one oppressed by the cares of government.*) People are generally contented and happy when they have gained their desires ; but kings have no sooner attained the object of their aspirations than all their troubles begin. (*Leans on the shoulders of his attendants, and ascends the throne* C.) RAIVATIKA, what can possible

be the message that the venerable Kanwa has
sent me by these hermits ?

WAR.　If you ask my opinion, Sire, I think the hermits
merely wish to take an opportunity of testifying their loyalty, and are therefore come to
offer homage to your majesty.

Enter the HERMITS, *leading* SHAKUNTALA, *attended by*
GAUTAMI ; SHARANGARAVA *and* SHARADVAT *and, in*
advance of them, the CHAMBERLAIN *and the* DOMESTIC
PRIEST.

CHAM.　This way, reverend sirs, this way.

PRIEST.　(*Pointing to the* KING.) Most reverend sirs,
there stands the protector of the four classes
of the people ; the guardian of the four orders
of the priesthood ³· He has just left the
judgment-seat, and is waiting for you.
Behold him !

SHARN.　Great Brámhan, we are happy in thinking that
the King's power is exerted for the protection
of all classes of his subjects. We have not
come as petitioners—we have the fullest confidence in the generosity of his nature.

WAR.　So please your majesty, I judge from the placid
countenance of the hermits that they have no
alarming message to deliver.

KING.　(*Looking at* SHAKUNTALA.) But the lady there—
Who can she be, whose form of matchless grace
Is half concealed beneath her flowing veil ?
Among the sombre hermits she appears.
Like a fresh bud'mid sear and yellow leaves.

WAR.　So please your majesty, my curiosity is also
roused, but no conjecture occurs to my mind.
This at least is certain, that she deserves to
be looked at more closely.

KING.　True ; but it is not right to gaze at another man's
wife ⁴·

SHAK.　(*placing her hand on her bosom. Aside.*) O my
heart, why this throbbing ? Remember thy
lord's affection, and take courage.

PRIEST.   (*Advancing.*) These holy men have been received with all due honour. One of them has now a message to deliver from his spiritual superior. Will your majesty deign to hear it ?

KING.   I am all attention

HER.   (*Extending their hands.*) Victory to the King !

KING.   I trust the venerable Kanwa is in good health. The world is interested in his well-being. Let me hear his commands.

SHARN.   He bade us say that he feels happy in giving his sanction to the marriage which your Majesty contracted with this lady, his daughter, privately and by mutual agreement. Because

By us thou art esteemed the most illustrious
Of noble husbands ; and Shakuntalá
Virtue herself in human form revealed.
Great Brahmá hath in equal yoke united
A bride unto a husband worthy of her :—
Henceforth let none make blasphemous complaint
That he is pleased with ill-assorted unions 5·

Since, therefore, she expects soon to be the mother of thy child, receive her into thy palace, that she may perform, in conjunction with thee, the ceremonies prescribed by religion on such an occasion.

SHAK.   (*Aside.*) Ah ! how I tremble for my lord's reply.

KING.   What strange proposal is this ?

SHAK.   (*Aside.*) His words are fire to me.

SHARN.   What do I hear ? Dost thou, then, hesitate ? Monarch, thou art well acquainted with the ways of the world, and knowest that

A wife, however virtuous and discreet,
If she live separate from her wedded lord,
Though under shelter of her parent's roof,
Is mark for vile suspicion. Let her dwell
Beside her husband, though he hold her not
In his affection. So her kinsmen will it.

KING. Do you really mean to assert that I ever married
         this lady ?

SHAK. (*Despondingly.   Aside.*) O my heart, thy
         worst misgivings are confirmed.

SHARN. Is it becoming in a monarch to depart from the
         rules of justice, because he repents of his
         engagements ?

KING. I cannot answer a question which is based on a
         mere fabrication.

SHARN. Such inconstancy is fortunately not common,
         excepting in men intoxicated by power.

KING. Is that remark aimed at me ?

GAU. Be not ashamed, my daughter. Let me remove
         thy veil for a little space. Thy husband will
         then recognize thee. (*Removes her veil.*)

KING. (*Gazing at* SHAKUNTALA. *Aside.*)
         What charms are here revealed before mine eyes !
         Truly no blemish mars the symmetry
         Of that fair form ; yet can I ne'er believe
         She is my wedded wife ; and like a bee
         That circles round the flower whose nectared cup
         Teems with the dew of morning, I must pause
         Ere eagerly I taste the proffered sweetness.
                        (*Remains wrapped in thought.*)

WAR. How admirably does our royal master's behaviour
         prove his regard for justice ! Who else would
         hesitate for a moment when good fortune
         offered for his acceptance a form of such rare
         beauty ?

SHARN. Greet King, why art thou silent ?

KING. Holy men, I have revolved the matter in my
         mind ; but the more I think of it, the less
         able am I to recollect that I ever contracted
         an alliance with this lady. What answer,
         then, can I possibly give you when I do not
         believe myself to be her husband, and I plainly
         see that she is soon to become a mother ?

SHAK. (*Aside.*) Woe ! woe ! Is our very marriage
         to be called in question by my own husband ?

Ah me ! is this to be the end of all my bright
visions of wedded happiness ?

SHARN.   Beware !

Beware how thou insult the holy Sage !
Remember how he generously allowed
Thy secret union with his foster-child :
And how, when thou didst rob him of his treasure,
He sought to furnish thee excuse, when rather
He should have cursed thee for a ravisher.

SHARD.   Shárngarava, speak to him no more. Shakuntalá
our part is performed ; we have said all we
had to say, and the King has replied in the
manner thou hast heard. It is now thy turn
to give him convincing evidence of thy
marriage.

SHAK.   (*Aside.*)   Since his feeling towards me has
undergone a complete revolution, what will
it avail to revive old recollections ? One
thing is clear—I shall soon have to mourn my
own widowhood. (*Aloud.*) My revered husband——   (*Stops short.*) But no—I dare
not address thee by this title, since thou hast
refused to acknowledge our union. Noble
descendant of Puru ! It is not worthy of
thee to betray an innocent-minded girl, and
disown her in such terms, after having so
lately and so solemnly plighted thy vows to
her in the hermitage.

KING.   (*Stopping his ears.*) I will hear no more. Be
such a crime far from my thoughts !
What evil spirit can possess thee, lady,
That thou dost seek to sully my good name
By base aspersions ?

SHAK.   If, then, thou really believest me to be the wife
of another, and thy present conduct proceeds
from some cloud that obscures thy recollection, I will easily convince thee by this token,

KING.   An excellent idea !

SHAK. (*Feeling for the ring.*) Alas ! alas ! woe is me ! There is no ring on my finger ! (*Looks with anguish at* GAUTAMI.)

GAU. The ring must have slipped off when thou wast in the act of offering homage to the holy water of Shachí's sacred pool, near Shakrávatára.

KING. (*Smiling.*) People may well talk of the readiness of woman's invention ! Here is an instance of it.

SHAK. Say, rather, of the omnipotence of fate. I will mention another circumstance, which may yet convince thee.

KING. By all means let me hear it at once.

SHAK. One day, while we were seated in a jasmine bower, thou didst pour into the hollow of thine hand some water, sprinkled by a recent shower in the cup of a lotus blossom——

KING. (*Interrupting.*) Voluptuaries may allow themselves to be seduced from the path of duty by falsehoods such as these, expressed in honeyed words.

SHAK. (*Angrily.*) Dishonorable man, thou judgest of others by thine own evil heart. Thou, at least, art unrivalled in perfidy, and standest alone—a base deceiver in the garb of virtue and religion—like a deep pit whose yawning mouth is concealed by smiling flowers.

KING. (*Aside.*) Her anger, at any rate, appears genuine, and makes me almost doubt whether I am in the right. (*Aloud.*) My good lady, Dushyanta's character is well known to all. I comprehend not your meaning.

SHAK. Well do I deserve to be thought a harlot for having, in the innocence of my heart, and out of the confidence I reposed in a Prince of Puru's race, entrusted my honour to a man whose mouth distils honey, while his hears it full of poison. (*Covers her face with her mantle, and bursts into tears.*)

SHARN. Thus is it that burning remorse must ever follow rash actions which might have been avoided, and for which one has only one's-self to blame.

Not hastily should marriage be contracted,
And specially in secret. Many a time,
In hearts that know not each the other's fancies,
Fond love is changed into most bitter hate.

KING. How now ! Do you give credence to this woman rather than to me, that you heap such accusations on me ?

SHARD. This altercation is idle, Shárngarava. We have executed the commission of our preceptor ; come let us return. (*To the* KING.)

Shakuntalá is certainly thy bride ;
Receive her or reject her, she is thine.
Do with her, King, according to thy pleasure—
The husband o'er the wife is absolute.

Go on before us, Gautami. (*They move away* L.)

SHAK. What ! is it not enough to have been betrayed by this perfidious man ? Must you also forsake me, regardless of my tears and lamentations ? (*Attempts to follow them.*)

GAU. (*Stopping.*) My son Shárngarava, see, Shakuntalá is following us, and with tears implores us not to leave her. Alas ! poor child, what will she do here with a cruel husband who casts her from him ?

SHARN. (*Turning angrily towards her.*) Wilful woman, dost thou seek to be independent of thy lord ? (SHAKUNTALA *trembles with fear.*)

Shakuntalá !

If thou art really what the King proclaims thee,
How can thy father e'er receive thee back
Into his house and home ? but, if thy conscience
Be witness to thy purity of soul,
E'en should thy husband to a handmaid's lot

Condemn thee, thou mayst cheerfully endure it,
When ranked among the number of his household.

      Thy duty, therefore, is to stay. As for us,
      we must return immediately. (*Exeunt all
      the* HERMITS *with* GOUTAMI.)

KING. (*To his* PRIEST.) You must counsel me, rever-
      ed sir, as to my course of action.

PRIEST. (*After deliberation.*) You must take an inter-
      mediate course.

KING. What course, revered sir ? Tell me at once.

PRIEST. I will provide an asylum for the lady in my own
      house until the birth of her child ; and my
      reason, if you ask me, is this : Soothsayers
      have predicted that your first-born will have
      universal dominion. Now, if the hermit's
      daughter bring forth a son with the discus or
      mark of empire in the lines of his hand, 6 you
      must admit her immediately into your royal
      apartments with great rejoicings ; if not, then
      determine to send her back as soon as possible
      to her father.

KING. I bow to the decision of my spiritual adviser.

PRIEST. Daughter, follow me.

SHAK. O divine earth, open and receive me into thy
      bosom ! (*Exit* SHAKUNTALA *weeping, with
      the* PRIEST. *In the interval she is carried
      up in the* HEAVENS. *The* KING *remains
      absorbed in thinking of her, though the
      curse still clouds his recollection.*)

OMNES. A miracle ! a miracle !

        A GRAND TABLEAU.

PRELUDE TO ACT VI.

SCENE.—*A Street.*

Enter the King's brother-in-law as SUPERINTENDENT *of the city police; and with him* TWO CONSTABLES, *dragging a poor* FISHERMAN, *who has his hands tied behind his back, armed with nets, hooks, and angles.*

2ND CONS. (*Striking the prisoner.*)   Take that for a rascally thief that you are ; and now tell us, sirrah, where you found this ring—aye, the King's own signet-ring.   See, here is the royal name engraved on the setting of the jewel.

FISH. (*With a gesture of alarm.*)   Mercy ! kind sirs, mercy !   I did not steal it ; indeed I did not.

1ST CONS.   Oh ! then I suppose the King took you for some fine Bráhman, and made you a present of it ?

FISH.   Only hear me.   I am but a poor fisherman, living at Shakrávatára——

2ND CONS.   Scoundrel, who ever asked you, pray, for a history of your birth and parentage ?

SUP. (*To one of the* CONSTABLES.)   Súchaka, let the fellow tell his own story from the beginning. Don't interrupt him.

2ND CONS.   As you please, master.   Go on, then, sirrah, and say what you've got to say.

FISH.   You see in me a poor man, who supports his family by catching fish with nets, hooks, and the like.

SUP. (*Laughing.*)   A most refined occupation, certainly !

FISH.   Blame me not for it, master.
>The father's occupation, though despised
>By others, casts no shame upon the son,
>And he should not forsake it. Is the priest
>Who kills the animal for sacrifice
>Therefore deemed cruel ? Sure a low-born man
>May, though a fisherman, be tender-hearted.

SUP.   Well, well ; go on with your story.

FISH.   One day I was cutting open a large carp I had
just hooked, when the sparkle of a jewel
caught my eye, and what should I find in the
fish's maw but that ring ! Soon afterwards,
when I was offering it for sale, I was seized
by your honours. Now you know everything.
Whether you kill me, or whether you let me
go, this is the true account of how the ring
came into my possession.

SUP.   (*To one of the* CONSTABLES.)   Well, Jánuka, the
rascal emits such a fishy odour that I have no
doubt of his being a fisherman ; but we must
inquire a little more closely into this queer
story about the ring. Come, we'll take him
to the King's household.

2ND CONS.   Very good, master. Get on with you, you
cutpurse. (*Exeunt* L.)

SCENE II.—*Frontage of the Palace.*

SUPERINTENDENT *and two* CONSTABLES *with the*
FISHERMAN *as their prisoner discovered* C.

SUP.   Now attend, Súchaka ; keep you guard here at the
gate ; and hark ye, sirrahs, take good care
your prisoner does not escape, while I go in
and lay the whole story of the discovery of
this ring before the King in person. I will
soon return and let you know his commands.
(*Exit* C. *door.*\

1ST CONS.   I say, Jánuka, I fancy the Superintendent
will be long time away.   4

2ND CONS. Aye, aye ; kings are not to be got at so
easily. Folks must bide the proper opportunity.

Re-enter SUPERINTENDENT C. *door.*

SUP. Ho, there, Súchaka ! set the fisherman at liberty,
I tell you. His story about the ring is all
correct.

1ST CONS. Oh ! very good, sir ; as you please.

2ND CONS. The fellow had one foot in the grave and
now here he is in the land of the living.
(*Releases him.*)

FISH. (*Bowing to the* SUPERINTENDENT.) Now, master, what think you of my way of getting a
livelihood ?

SUP. Here my good man, the king desired me to
present you with this purse. It contains a
sum of money equal to the full value of
the ring. (*Gives him the money.*)

FISH. (*Taking it and bowing.*) His majesty does me
too great honour.

1ST CONS. You may well say so. He might as well
have taken you from the gallows to seat you
on his state elephant. (*Exeunt,* R.)

ACT VI.

SCENE.—*The Garden of the Palace.*

*Two Maidens discovered keeping guard over the
Garden.*

Enter CHAMBERLAIN, R.

CHAM. Well then, now you know it, take care you
don't continue your preparations.

1st MAI. But tell us, kind sir, why has the King prohibited the usual festivities ? We are curious to hear, if we may.

CHAM. The whole affair is now public ; why I should
not speak of it ! Has not the gossip about
the king's rejection of Shakuntalá reached
your ears yet ?

2ND MAI. Oh yes, we heard the story from the king's
brother-in-law, as far, at least, as the discovery
of the ring.

CHAM. Then there is little more to tell you. As soon
as the king's memory was restored by the
sight of his own ring, he exclaimed, ' Yes,
it is all true. I remember now my secret
marriage with Shakuntalá. When I repudi-
ated her, I had lost my recollection.' Ever
since that moment, he has yielded himself a
prey to the bitterest remorse.

He loathes his former pleasures ; he rejects
The daily homage of his ministers.
On his lone couch he tosses to and fro,
Courting repose in vain. Whene'er he meets
The ladies of his palace, and would fain
Address them with politeness, he confounds
Their names ; or calling them 'Shakuntalá,'
Is straightway silent and abashed with shame.

     In short, the king is so completely out of his
mind that the festival has been prohibited.

(*Listening.*) Oh! here comes his majesty in this direction. Pass on, maidens ; attend to your
duties. (*Exeunt* L.)

Enter King DUSHYANTA, *dressed in deep mourning,
attended by his Jester,* MATHAVYA, R.

KING. (*Walking slowly up and down in deep thought.*)
When fatal lethargy o'erwhelmed my soul,
My loved one strove to rouse me, but in vain :
And now when I would fain in slumber deep
Forget myself, full soon remorse doth wake me.

MATH. (*Aside.*) He is taken with another attack of
this odius Shakuntalá fever. How shall we
ever cure him ?

Re-enter CHAMBERLAIN. R.

CHAM. Victory to the King ! Great Prince, the royal
pleasure-grounds have been put in order.
Your majesty can resort to them for exercise
and amusement whenever you think proper.

KIN . Váčayan tell the worthy Pishuna, my prime minis-
ter, from me, that I am so exhausted by
want of sleep that I cannot sit on the judgment-seat to-day. If any case of importance
be brought before the tribunal he must give
it his best attention, and inform me of the circumstances by letter. (*Exit* CHAMBERLAIN R.)

MATH. Now that you have rid yourself of these troublesome fellows, you can enjoy the delightful
coolness of your pleasure-grounds without
interruption.

KING. Ah ! my dear friend, there is an old adage—
'When affliction has a mind to enter, she will
find a crevice somewhere;' and it is verified
in me. Oh ! my dear friend, how vividly all
the circumstances of my union with Shakuntalá present themselves to my recollection at
this moment ! But tell me now, how it was
that, between the time of my leaving her in
the hermitage and my subsequent rejection of
her, you never breathed her name to me?
True, you were not by my side when I dis-
owned her ; but I had confided to you the
story of my love and you were acquainted
with every particular. Did it pass out of
your mind as it did out of mine ?

MATH. No, no ; trust me for that. But, if you remember, when you had finished telling me
about it, you added that I was not to take the
story in earnest, for that you were not really

in love with a country girl, but were only
jesting; and I was dull and thick-headed
enough to believe you. But so fate decreed,
and there is no help for it.

KING. My dear friend, suggest some relief for my misery.

MATH. Come, come, cheer up; why do you give way?
Such weakness is unworthy of you. Great
men never surrender themselves to uncon-
trolled grief. Do not mountains remain un-
shaken even in a gale of wind?

KING. How can I be otherwise than inconsolable, when
I call to mind the agonised demeanour of the
dear one on the occasion of my disowning her?

MATH. An idea has just struck me. I should not
wonder if some celestial being had carried
her off to heaven.

KING. Very likely. Who else would have dared to lay
a finger on a wife, the idol of her husband?
It is said that Menaká, the nymph of heaven
gave her birth. The suspicion has certainly
crossed my mind that some of her celestial
companions may have taken her to their own
abode.

MATH. If that's the case, you will be certain to meet her
before long.

KING. Why?

MATH. No father and mother can endure to see a
daughter suffering the pain of separation from
her husband.

KING. Oh! my dear Mathavya,

Was it a dream? or did some magic dire,
Dulling my senses with a strange delusion,
O'ercome my spirit? or did destiny,
Jealous of my good actions, mar their fruit,
And rob me of their guerdon? It is past,
Whate'er the spell that bound me. Once again
Am I awake, but only to behold
The precipice o'er which my hopes have fallen.

MATH.   Do not despair in this manner. Is not this very
ring a proof that what has been lost may be
unexpectedly found?

KING.   (*Gazing at the Ring.*) Ah! this ring, too, has
fallen from a station which it will not easily
regain, and deserves all my sympathy.

MATH.   Pray, how did the ring ever come upon her hand
at all?

KING.   You shall hear. When I was leaving my beloved
Shakuntalá that I might return to my own
capital, she said to me, with tears in her eyes,
'How long will it be ere my lord send for me
to his palace and make me his queen?

MATH.   Well, what was your reply?

KING.   Then I placed the ring on her finger, and thus
addressed her—

> Repeat each day one letter of the name
> Engraven on this gem ; ere thou hast reckoned
> The tale of syllables, my minister
> Shall come to lead thee to thy husband's palace.

But, hard-hearted man that I was, I forgot to fulfil
my promise, owing to the infatuation that
took possession of me.

MATH.   But how did the ring contrive to pass into the
stomach of that carp which the fisherman
caught and was cutting up?

KING.   It must have slipped from my Shakuntalá's hand,
and fallen into the stream of the Ganges,
while she was offering homage to the water of
Shachí's holy pool.

MATH.   Very likely.

KING.   Let me now address a few words of reproof to
this ring.

MATH.   (*Aside.*) He is going stark mad, I verily believe

KING.   Hear me, thou dull and undiscerning bauble!
For so it argues thee, that thou couldst leave
The slender fingers of her hand, to sink
Beneath the waters. Yet what marvel is it

That thou shouldst lack discernment ? let me rather
Heap curses on myself, who, though endowed
With reason, yet rejected her I loved.

MATH.   (*Aside.*)   And so, I suppose, I must stand here
to be devoured by hunger, whilst he goes on
in this sentimental strain.

KING.   O forsaken one, unjustly banished from my presence, take pity on thy slave, whose heart is
consumed by the fire of remorse, and return
to my sight.

Enter ATTENDANT *hurriedly, with a picture in his
hand.* R

ATT.   (*Showing the picture.*)   Here is the Queen's
portrait.

MATH.   Excellent, my dear friend, excellent ! The imi-
tation of nature is perfect, and the attitude of
the figures is really charming. They stand
out in such bold relief that the eye is quite
deceived.

KING.   I own 'tis not amiss, though it pourtrays
But feebly her angelic loveliness.
Aught less than perfect is depicted falsely,
And fancy must supply the imperfection.

MATH.   Tell me,—I see three female figures drawn on
the canvas, and all of them beautiful ; which
of the three is her majesty, Shakuntalá.

KING.   Which should you imagine to be intended for her ?

MATH.   She who is leaning, apparently a little tired,
against the stem of that mango-tree, the
tender leaves of which glitter with the water
she has poured upon them. Her arms are
gracefully extended ; her face is somewhat
flushed with the heat ; and a few flowers
have escaped from her hair, which has become
unfastened, and hangs in loose tresses about
her neck. That must be the Queen Shakuntalá, and the others, I presume, are her two
attendants.

KING. I congratulate you on your discernment. Behold the proof of my passion ;—Attendant.—The garden in the back-ground of the picture is only half-painted. Go, fetch the brush that I may finish it.

ATT. Worthy Màthavya, have the kindness to hold the picture until I return.

KING. (*Takes the picture.*) Nay, I will hold it myself.

(Exit ATTENDANT, R.)

My loved one came but lately to my presence
And offered me herself, but in my folly
I spurned the gift, and now I fondly cling
To her mere image ; even as a madman
Would pass the waters of the gushing stream,
And thirst for airy vapours of the desert.[1]

MATH. He has been fool enough to forego the reality for the semblance, the substance for the shadow. (*Aloud.*) Tell us, I pray, what else remains to be painted.

KING. You shall hear—

I wish to see the Màlinì pourtrayed,
Its tranquil course by banks of sand impeded :
Upon the brink a pair of swans : beyond,
The hills adjacent to Himàlaya,
Studded with deer ; and, near the spreading shade
Of some large tree, where 'mid the branches hang
The hermits' vests of bark, a tender doe,
Rubbing its downy forehead on the horn
Of a black antelope, should be depicted.

MATH. (*Aside.*) Pooh! if I were he, I would fill up the vacant spaces with a lot of grizzly-bearded old hermits.

KING. My dear Màthavya, there is still a part of Shakuntalà's dress which I purposed to draw, but I find I have omitted.

MATH. What is that ?

KING.   A sweet Sirísha blossom should be twined
Behind her ear, its perfumed crest depending
Towards her cheek ; and, resting on her bosom,
A lotus-fibre necklace, soft and bright
As an autumnal moon-beam, should be traced.

MATH.   Pray, why does the Queen cover her lips with
the tips of her fingers, bright as the blossom
of a lily, as if she were afraid of something ?
(*Looking more closely*).   Oh ! I see ; a
vagabond bee, intent on thieving the honey of
flowers, has mistaken her mouth for a rose-
bud, and is trying to settle upon it.

KING.   A bee ! drive off the impudent insect, will you ?

MATH.   That's your business.   Your royal prerogative
gives you power over all offenders.

KING.   Very true.   Listen to me, thou favourite guest of
flowering plants ; why   give   thyself   the
trouble of hovering here ?

See where thy partner sits on yonder flower,
And waits for thee ere she will sip its dew.

MATH.   You'll find the obstinate creature is not to be
sent about his business so easily as you think.

KING.   Dost thou presume to disobey ?   Now hear me—
An thou but touch the lips of my beloved,
Sweet as the opening blossom, whence I quaffed
In happier days love's nectar, I will place thee
Within the hollow of yon lotus cup,
And there imprison thee for thy presumption.

MATH.   He must be bold indeed not to show any fear
when you threaten him with such an awful
punishment.   (*Smiling, aside*).   He is stark
mad, that's clear ; and I believe, by keeping
him company, I am beginning to talk almost
as wildly.   (*Aloud.*)   Look, it is only a
painted bee.

KING.   Painted ! impossible !   Oh ! my dear friend, why
were you so ill-natured as to tell me the
truth ?   Alas ! my dear Màthavya, why am I

doomed to be the victim of perpetual dis-
appointment ?

Re-enter ATTENDANT, R.

ATT.   Victory to the King ! I was coming along with
the box of colours in my hand——

KING.   What now ?

ATT.   When I met the Queen Vasumatí, attended by
Taraliká. She insisted on taking it from me,
and declared she would herself deliver it into
your Majesty's hands.

MATH.   By what luck did you contrive to escape her ?

ATT.   While her maid was disengaging her mantle,
which had caught in the branch of a shrub,
I ran away.

KING.   Here, my good friend, take the picture and conceal it. My attentions to the Queen have
made her presumptuous. She will be here in
a minute.

MATH.   Conceal the picture ! conceal myself, you mean
(*Getting up and taking the picture*). The
Queen has a bitter draught in store for you,
which we will have to swallow as Shiva did
the poison at the Deluge.[2] When you are
well quit of her, you may send and call me
from the Palace of Clouds,[3] where I shall
take refuge. (*Exit, running* L.)

KING.   Alas ! the shades of my forefathers are even now
beginning to be alarmed, lest at my death
they may be deprived of their funeral libations.

Enter MATALI (*descending from the heavens in the
car of* INDRA)

(*Putting back his arrow.*) What, Mátali !
Welcome, most noble charioteer of the mighty
Indra.

MAT.   There is a race of giants, the descendants of
Kálanemi,[4] whom the gods find difficult to
subdue.

KING.   So I have already heard from Nárada.[5]

MAT. Heaven's mighty lord, who deigns to call thee 'friend,'
   Appoints thee to the post of highest honour,
   As leader of his armies ; and commits
   The subjugation of this giant brood
   To thy resistless arms, e'en as the sun
   Leaves the pale moon to dissipate the darkness.

    Let your Majesty, therefore, ascend at once
    the celestial car of Indra ; and, grasping your
    arms, advance to victory.

KING. The mighty Indra honours me too highly by such
   a mark of distinction. . (*Exeunt, ascending in
   the sky.*)

ACT VII.

SCENE.—*The Sky.*

King DUSHYANTA *and* MATALI *in the car of*
INDRA, *discovered moving in the air.*

KING. Tell me, Mátali, what is that range of mountains
   which, like a bank of clouds illumined by the
   setting sun, pours down a stream of gold ?
   On one side its base dips into the eastern
   ocean, and on the other into the western.

MAT. Great Prince, it is called 'Golden-peak,' and
   is the abode of the attendants of the god of
   Wealth. In this spot the highest forms of
   penance are wrought out by the great Kashyap.

KING. Then I must not neglect so good an opportunity
   of obtaining his blessings. I should much like
   to visit this venerable personage and offer him
   my homage.

MAT. By all means. An excellent idea ! (*Guides the
   car to the earth.*)

KING. (*In a tone of wonder.*) How's this ?

Our chariot wheels move noiselessly. Around
No clouds of dust arise ; no shock betokened
Our contact with the earth ; we seem to glide
Above the ground, so lightly do we touch it.

MATALI.   Such is the difference between the car of Indra
            and that of your majesty. Descend great
            King.

KING.   As you think proper. (*Descends.*)

MAT.   Great King, I go. (*Exit in the sky.*)

KING.   (*Feeling his arm throb.*)

Wherefore this causeless throbbing, O mine arm ?
All hope has fled for ever ; mock me not
With presages of good, when happiness
Is lost, and nought but misery remains.

A VOICE WITHIN. Be not so naughty. Do you begin
            already to show a refractory spirit ?

KING.   (*Listening.*) This is no place for petulance.
            Who can it be whose behaviour calls for such
            a rebuke ? (*Looking in the direction of the
            sound and smiling.*) A child, is it ? closely
            attended by two holy women. His disposition
            seems anything but child-like. See,

He braves the fury of yon vicious animal
Suckling its savage offspring, and compels
The angry whelp to leave the half-sucked dug,
Tearing its tender mane in boisterous sport.

Enter a CHILD, *attended by* TWO ATTENDANTS *and
two holy women, of the hermitage, with a Puppy in
his hand,* L.

CHILD.   Open your mouth, my young whelp I want to
            count your teeth.

1ST ATT.   You naughty child, why do you teaze the
            animal ?

KING.   Strange ! My heart inclines towards the boy
            with almost as much affection as if he were
            my own child. What can be the reason ? I
            suppose my own childlessness makes me yearn
            towards the sons of others.

2ND ATT. That animal will certainly attack you if you do
          not release her whelp.

CHILD. (*Laughing.*) Oh! indeed! let her come. Much
          I fear her, to be sure! (*Pouts his under-lip
          in defiance.*)

KING. The germ of mighty courage lies concealed
          Within this noble infant, like a spark
          Beneath the fuel, waiting but a breath
          To fan the flame and raise a conflagration.

1ST ATT. Let the young whelp go, like a dear child, and
          I will give you something else to play with.

CHILD. Where is it? Give it me first. (*Stretches out
          his hand.*)

KING. (*Looking at his hand.*) How's this? His hand
          exhibits one of those mystic marks which
          are the sure prognostic of universal empire.

2ND ATT. We shall never pacify him by mere words.
          Be kind enough to go to my cottage, and you
          will find there a plaything belonging to Már-
          kándeya, one of the hermit's children. It is
          a peacock made of China-ware, painted in
          many colours. Bring it here for the child.

1ST ATT. Very well. (*Exit L.*)

CHILD. No, no; I shall go on playing with the young
          puppy. (*Looks at the* ATTENDANT *and
          laughs.*)

KING. I feel an unaccountable affection for this wayward
          child.
          How blessed the virtuous parents whose attire
          Is soiled with dust, by raising from the ground
          The child that asks a refuge in their arms!
          And happy are they while with lisping prattle,
          In accents sweetly inarticulate,
          He charms their ears; and with his artless smiles
          Gladdens their hearts, revealing to their gaze
          His tiny teeth just budding into view.

2ND ATT. I see how it is. He pays me no manner
          of attention.

KING.   (*Approaching and smiling.*)   Listen to me, thou child of a mighty saint.

2ND ATT.   Gentle sir, I thank you ; but he is not the saint's son.

KING.   His behaviour and whole bearing would have led me to doubt it, had not the place of his abode encouraged the idea. (*Follows the child, and takes him by the hand. Aside.*)

I marvel that the touch of this strange child
Should thrill me with delight ; if so it be,
How must the fond caresses of a son
Transport the father's soul who gave him being.

2ND ATT.   (*Looking at them both.*)   Wonderful ! Prodigious !

KING.   What excites your surprise, my good man ?

2ND ATT.   I am astonished at the striking resemblance between the child and yourself.

KING.   (*Fondling the child.*)   If he be not the son of the great sage, of what family does he come, may I ask ?

2ND ATT.   Of the race of Puru.

KING.   (*Aside.*)   What ! are we, then, descended from the same ancestry ? This, no doubt, accounts for the resemblance he traces between the child and me. (*Aloud.*) But how could mortals by their own power gain admission to this sacred region ?

2ND ATT.   Your remark is just ; but your wonder will cease when I tell you that his mother is the offspring of a celestial nymph, and gave him birth in the hallowed grove of Káshyapa.

KING.   (*Aside.*)   Strange that my hopes should be again excited ! (*Aloud.*) But what, let me ask, was the name of the prince whom she deigned to honour with her hand ?

2ND ATT.   How could I think of polluting my lips by. the mention of a wretch who had the cruelty to desert his lawful wife ?

KING.   (*Aside.*)   Ha ! the description suits me exactly
         Would I could bring myself to inquire the
         name of the child's mother ! (*Reflecting.*)
         But it is against propriety to make too minute
         inquiries about the wife of another man.

Re-Enter FIRST ATTENDANT *with the china peacock
         in his hand*

1ST ATT. Sarva-damana, Sarva-damana, see, see, what
          a beautiful Shakunta.

CHILD.   (*Looking round.*) My mother ! Where ? Let
          me go to her.

2ND ATT. He mistook the word Shakunta for Shakuntalá.
          The boy dotes upon his mother, and she is
          ever uppermost in his thoughts.

1ST ATT. Nay, my dear child, I said, look at the beauty
          of this Shakunta.

KING.   (*Aside.*)   What ! is his mother's name Shakun-
          talá ?   But the name is not uncommon among
          women.   Alas ! I fear the mere similarity of
          a name, like the deceitful vapour of the
          desert, has once more raised my hopes only
          to dash them to the ground.

CHILD.   What a beautiful peacock ! (*Takes the toy.*)

1ST ATT. (*Looking at the child. In great distress.*) Alas !
          alas !   I do not see the amulet on his wrist.

KING.   Don't distress yourself.   Here it is.   It fell off
          while he was struggling with the young brute
          (*Stoops to pick it up.*)

2ND ATT. Hold ! hold !   Touch it not, for your life.
          How marvellous !   He has actually taken it
          up without the slightest hesitation. (*Both
          raise their hands to their breasts and look at
          each other in astonishment.*)

KING.   Why did you try to prevent my touching it ?

1ST ATT. Listen, great Monarch.   This amulet, known
          as ' The Invincible,' was given to the boy by
          the divine son of Maríchi, soon after his
          birth, when the natal ceremony was perform-
          ed.   Its peculiar virtue is, that when it falls

on the ground, no one excepting the father or mother of the child can touch it unhurt.

KING.   And suppose another person touches it ?

1ST ATT.   Then it instantly becomes a serpent, and bites him.

KING.   Have you ever witnessed the transformation with your own eyes ?

2ND ATT.   Over and over again.

KING.   (*With rapture. Aside.*) Joy ! joy ! Are then my dearest hopes to be fulfilled ? (*Embraces the child.*)

Enter SHAKUNTLA, *in widow's apparel, with her long hair twisted into a single braid,* L.

SHAK.   (*Aside.*)   I have just heard that Sarva-damana's amulet has retained its form, though a stranger raised it from the ground. I can hardly believe in my good fortune. Yet why should not Sánumatí's prediction be verified ?

KING.   (*Gazing at* SHAKUNTALA.)   Alas ! can this indeed be my Shakuntalá ?

Clad in the weeds of widowhood, her face
Emaciate with fasting, her long hair
Twined in a single braid,[1] her whole demeanour
Expressive of her purity of soul :
With patient constancy she thus prolongs
The vow to which my cruelty condemned her.

SHAK.   (*Gazing at the* KING, *who is pale with remorse.*) Surely this is not like my husband ; yet who can it be that dares pollute by the pressure of his hand my child, whose amulet should protect him from a stranger's touch ?

CHILD.   (*Going to his mother.*) Mother, who is this man that has been kissing me and calling me his son ?

KING.   My best beloved, I have indeed treated thee most cruelly, but am now once more thy fond and affectionate lover. Refuse not to acknowledge ? as thy husband ?

SHAK.   (*Aside.*) Be of good cheer, my heart. The
           anger of Destiny is at last appeased. Heaven
           regards thee with compassion. But is he in
           very truth my husband ?

KING.   Behold me, best and loveliest of women,
           Delivered from the cloud of fatal darkness
           That erst oppressed my memory. Again
           Behold us brought together by the grace
           Of the great lord of Heaven. So the moon
           Shines forth from dim eclipse,[2] to blend his rays
           With the soft lustre of his Rohiní.

SHAK.   May my husband be victorious——(*She stops
           short, her voice choked with tears.*)

KING.   O fair one, though the utterance of thy prayer
           Be lost amid the torrent of thy tears,
           Yet does the sight of thy fair countenance,
           And of thy pallid lips, all unadorned [3]
           And colourless in sorrow for my absence,
           Make me already more than conqueror.

CHILD.   Mother, who is this man ?

SHAK.   My child, ask the Deity that presides over thy
           destiny.

KING.   (*Falling at* SHAKUNTALA's *feet.*)
       Fairest of women, banish from thy mind
       The memory of my cruelty ; reproach
       The fell delusion that o'erpowered my soul,
       And blame not me, thy husband ;' tis the curse
       Of him in whom the power of darkness[4] reigns,
       That he mistakes the gifts of those he loves
       For deadly evils. Even though a friend
       Should wreathe a garland on a blind man's brow
       Will he not cast it from him as a serpent ?

SHAK.   Rise, my own husband, rise. Thou wast not to
           blame. My own evil deeds, committed in a
           former state of being, brought down this
           judgment upon me. How else could my
           husband who was ever of a compassionate
           disposition, have acted so unfeelingly? (*The*

King rises.)   But tell me, my husband, how did the remembrance of thine unfortunate wife return to thy mind ?

KIN.   As soon as my heart's anguish is removed, and its wounds are healed, I will tell thee all. (*Wipes away the tears.*)

SHAK.   (*Seeing the signet-ring on his finger.*)   Ah! my dear husband, is that the Lost Ring ?

KING.   Yes ; the moment I recovered it, my memory was restored.

SHAK.   The ring was to blame in allowing itself to be lost at the very time when I was anxious to convince my noble husband of the reality of my marriage.

KING.   Receive it back, as the beautiful twining plant receives again its blossom in token of its re-union with the spring.

SHAK.   Nay ; I can never more place confidence in it. Let my husband retain it.

Enter MATALI R.

MAT.   I congratulate your Majesty.   Happy are you in your reunion with your wife : happy are you in beholding the face of your own son. Great King, let us pay our respectful visits to the venerable Kashyapa.

KING.   By all means. (*Exeunt,* R.)

SCENE II.—*The sacred grove.*

KASHYAPA *is discovered seated on a throne with his wife Aditi,* C.

Enter KING, SHAKUNTALA *her child, and* MATALI R, *accompanied by the two male attendants.*

KING   (*Prostrating himself.*)   Most august of beings Dushyanta, content to have fulfilled the commands of your son Indra, offers you his adoration.

KAS.   My son, long may'st thou live, and happily may'st thou reign over the earth !

SHAK.   I also prostrate myself before you, most adorable
        beings, and my child with me.

KAS.   My daughter,
    Thy lord resembles Indra, and thy child
    Is noble as Jayanta, Indra's son ;
    I have no worthier blessing left for thee,
    May'st thou be faithful as the god's own wife !

KING.   Most venerable Kashyapa, by your favour all my
        desires were accomplished even before I was
        admitted to your presence.   Never was mortal
        so honoured that his boon should be granted
        ere it was solicited. What other can I desire ?
        If, however, you permit me to form an other
        wish, I would humbly beg that the saying
        of the sage Bharata[5] be fulfilled :

    May kings reign only for their subjects' weal !
    May the divine Saraswati,[6] the source
    Of speech, and goddess of dramatic art,
    Be ever honoured by the great and wise !
    And may the purple self-existent god[7]
    Whose vital Energy[8] pervades all space,
    From future transmigration save my soul !

NOTES.

ACT I.

1. Shiva is called Pinakin, that is, "armed with a trident;" or, according to some, a bow named Pinaka. Shiva, not being invited to Daksha's sacrifice, was so indignant, that, with his wife, he suddenly presented himself, confounded the sacrifice, dispersed the gods, and chasing Yajna, 'the lord of sacrifice,' who fled in the form of a deer, overtook and decapitated him.

2. See Dushyanta's pedigree detailed at page xxiv. of the introduction (original Text).

3. The sage Kanwa was a descendant of Kashyap, whom the Hindus consider to have been the father of the inferior gods, demons, man, fish, reptiles, and all animals, by his twelve wives. Kanwa was the chief of a number of devotees, or hermits, who had constructed a hermitage on the banks of the river Malini, and surrounded it with gardens and groves, where penitential rites were performed, and animals were reared for sacrificial purposes, or for the amusement of the inmates.

4. A place of pilgrimage in the west of India, on the coast of Gujarat, near the temple of Somanath, or Somnat, made notorious by its gates, which were brought back from Ghizni by Lord Ellenborough's orders in 1842, and are now to be seen in the arsenal at Agra.

5. A quivering sensation in the right arm was supposed by the Hindús to prognosticate union with a beautiful woman. Throbbings of the arm or eyelid, if felt on the right side, were omens of good fortune in men ; if on the left, bad omens. The reverse was true of women.

6. The Keshara tree (*Mimusops elengi*), is the same as the Bakula, frequent mention of which is made in some of the Puránas. It bears a strong-smelling flower, which, according to Sir W. Jones, is ranked among the flowers of the Hindú paradise. The tree is very ornamental in pleasure-grounds.

7. Water for the feet is one of the first things invariably provided for a guest in all Eastern countries. Compare Genesis, xxiv. 32 ; Luke, vii. 44.

8. In the Ramayana, the great sage Vishwamitra (both king and saint), who raised himself by his austerities from the regal to the Bra. mhanical caste, is said to be the son of Gadhi, King of Kanuj, grandson of Kushanátha, and great grandson of Kushika or Kusha. On his accession to the throne, in the room of his father Gádhi, in the course of a tour through his dominions, he visited the hermitage of the sage Vasishtha, where the Cow of Plenty, a cow granting all desires, excited his cupidity. He offered the sage untold treasures for the cow ; but being refused, prepared to take it by force. A long war ensued between the king and the sage, (symbolical of the struggles between the military and Bráhmanical classes), which ended in the defeat of Vishwamitra, whose vexation was such, that he devoted himself to austerities in the hope of attaining the condition of a Bráhman.

9. This grass was held sacred by the Hindus, and was abundantly used in all their religious ceremonies. Its leaves are very long, and taper to a sharp needle-like point, of which the extreme acuteness was proverbial ; whence the epithet applied to a clever man, ' Sharp as the point of Kushagrass.' Its botanical name is *Poa cynosuroides.*

10. A species of Jhintí, or Barleria, with purple flowers, and covered with sharp prickles.

ACT II.

1. Who these women were has not been accurately ascertained. Yavana is properly Arabia, but is also a name applied to Greece. The Yavana women were therefore either natives of Arabia or Greece, and their business was to attend upon the king, and take charge of his weapons, especially his bows and arrows.

2. The doctrine of the transmigration of the soul from one body to another is an essential dogma of the Hindu religion, and connected with it is the belief in the power which every human being possesses of laying up for himself a store of merit by good deeds performed in the present or former births.

3. Dushyanta was a Rájarshi ; that is, a man of the military class who had attained the rank of Royal Sage or Saint by the practice of religious austerities. The title of Royal or Imperial Saint was only one degree inferior to that of a saint. Compare note 8, Act I.

4. The religious rites and sacrifices of holy men were often disturbed by certain evil spirits or goblins called Rakshasas, who were
the determined enemies of piety and devotion.

5. Vishnu, the Preserver, was one of the three principal gods. He
became incarnate in various forms for the good of mortals, and is the
great enemy of the demons.

6. The story of this monarch is told in the Rámáyana. He is
there described as a just and pious prince of the solar race, who as-
pired to celebrate a great sacrifice, hoping thereby to ascend to heav-
en in his mortal body. After various failures, he had recourse to
Vishwámitra, who undertook to conduct the sacrifice, and invited all
the gods to be present. They, however, refused to attend; upon
which the enraged Vishwámitra, by his own power, transported
Trishanku to the skies, whither he had no sooner arrived than he was
hurled down again by Indra and the gods ; but being arrested in his
downward course by the sage, he remained suspended between heaven
and earth, forming a canstellation in the southern hemisphere.

ACT III.

1. The Hindu Cupid, or god of love (Kama), is armed with a bow
made of sugar-cane, the string of which consists of bees. He has
five arrows, each tipped with blossom of a flower, which pierce the
heart through the five senses ; and his favourite arrow is pointed with
the *chuta*, or mango-flower.

2. That is, the male and female of the Chakra-vaka, commonly
called Chakwa and Chakwi, or Brahmani duck (*Anas casarca*). These
birds associate together during the day, and are, like turtle-doves,
patterns of connubial affection : but the legend is, that they are
doomed to pass the night apart, in consequence of a curse pronounced
upon them by a saint whom they had offended. As soon as night
commences, they take up their station on the opposite banks of a
river, and call to each other in piteous cries. The Bengalis consider
their flesh to be a good medicine for fever.

ACT IV.

1. Fire was an important object of veneration with the Hindus,
as with the ancient Persians. Perhaps the chief worship recom-
mended in the Vedas is that of Fire and the Sun. The holy fire was

deposited in a hallowed part of the house, or in a sacred building, and kept perpetually burning. Every morning and evening, oblations were offered to it by dropping clarified butter into the flame, accompanied with prayers and invocations.

2. Literally, 'as the Shami-tree is pregnant with fire.' The legend is, that the goddess Párvatí being one day under the influence of love, reposed on a trunk of this tree, whereby a sympathetic warmth was generated in the pith or interior of the wood, which ever after broke into a sacred flame on the slightest attrition.

3. The ancient Delhi, situated on the Ganges, and the capital of Dushyanta. Its site is about fifty miles from the modern Dehli, which is on the Jumna.

4. That is, the soles of her feet. It was customary for Hindu ladies to stain the soles of their feet of a red colour with the dye made from lac, a minute insect, bearing some resemblance to the cochineal.

5. Sharmishtha was the daughter of Vrisha-parvan, king of the demons, and wife of Yayati, son of Nahusha, one of the princes of the lunar dynasty, and ancestor of Dushyanta. Puru was the son of Yayati, by Sharmishtha.

6. At a sacrifice, sacred fires were lighted at the four cardinal points, and Kusha--grass was scattered around each fire.

7. The sandal is a large kind of myrtle with pointed leaves (*Sirium myrtifolium*). The wood affords many highly esteemed perfumes, unguents, &c., and is celebrated for its delicious scent. It is chiefly found on the slopes of the Malaya mountain or Western Ghauts on the Malabar coast. The roots of the tree are said to be infested with snakes. Indeed it seems to pay dearly for the fragrance of its wood : 'The root is infested by serpents, the blossoms by bees, the branches by monkeys, the summit by bears. In short, there is not a part of the sandal-tree that is not occupied by the vilest impurities.'—Hitopadesha, verse 162.

8. 'When the father of a family perceives his own wrinkles and grey hair, committing the care of his wife to his son, or accompanied by her, let him repair to the woods and become a hermit.'—Manu, VI., 2. It was usual for kings, at a certain time of life, to abdicate the throne in favour of the heir-apparent, and pass the remainder of their days in seclusion.

ACT V.

1. The attendant on the women's apartment. He is generally a Brahmin, and usually appears in the plays as a tottering and decrepit old man, leaning on his staff of office.

2. Compare note 1. Act IV.

3. The most remarkable feature in the Hindu social system, as depicted in the plays, was the division of the people into four classes or castes :—

1st. The sacerdotal, consisting of the Brahmans.—2nd. The military, consisting of fighting men, and including the king himself and the royal family. This class enjoyed great privileges, and must have been practically the most powerful.—3rd. The commercial, including merchants and husbandmen.—4th. The servile, consisting of servants and slaves. Of these four divisions the first alone has been preserved in its purity to the present day, although the Rajputs claim to be the representatives of the second class.

4. The Hindús were very careful to screen their wives from the curiosity of strangers ; and their great lawgiver, Manu, enjoined that married women should be cautiously guarded by their husband in the inner apartments (*antahpura*) appropriated to women (called by the Mohamadans Haram, and in common parlance in India *andar-mahall.*)

5. The god Brahma seems to have enjoyed a very unfortunate notoriety as taking pleasure in ill-assorted marriages, and encouraging them by his own example in the case of his own daughter.

6. When the lines of the right hand formed themselves into a circle, it was thought to be the mark of a future hero or emperor.

7. Shakra is a name of the god Indra, and Shakravatara is a sacred place of pilgrimage where he descended upon earth. Shachi is his wife to whom a *tirtha*, or holy bathing-place, was probably consecrated at the place where Shakuntala had performed her ablutions. Compare Note 4. Act I.

ACT VI.

1. A kind of mirage floating over waste places, and appearing at a distance like water. Travellers and some animals, especially deer, are supposed to be attracted and deceived by it.

2. At the churning of the ocean, after the Deluge, by the gods and demons, for the recovery or production of fourteen sacred things,

...adly poison called Kala-kuta, of Hala-hala, was generated so, ...lent that it would have destroyed the world, had not the god ...iva swallowed it. Its only effect was to leave a dark blue mark on his throat, whence his name Nilakantha. This name is also given to a beautiful bird, not wholly unlike our jay, common in Bengal.

3. The palace of king Dushyanta, so called because it was lofty as the clouds.

4. A Daitya or demon, with a hundred arms and as many heads.

5. A celebrated divine sage, usually reckoned among the ten patriarchs first created by Brahma. He acted as a messenger of the gods.

ACT VII.

1. The Hindu women collect their hair into a single long braid as a sign of mourning, when their husbands are dead or absent for a long period.

2. The following is the Hindu notion of an eclipse :—A certain demon, which had the tail of a dragon, was decapitated by Wishnu at the churning of the ocean ; but, as he had previously tasted of the Amrit or nectar reproduced at that time, he was thereby rendered immortal, and his head and tail, retaining their separate existence, when transferred to the stellar sphere. The head was called Ráhu, and became the cause of eclipses, by endeavouring at various times to swallow the sun and moon. So in the ' Hitopadesha,' line 192, the moon is said to be eaten by Rahu.

3. That is from the absence of colouring or paint.

4. According to the Hindú philosophy there were three qualities or properties incident to the state of humanity, viz: 1. Sattwa, 'excellence' or ' goodness' (quiescence), whence proceed truth, knowledge, purity, etc. 2. Rajas, ' passion' or ' foulness' (activity), which produces lust, pride, falsehood, etc., and is the cause of pain. 3. Tamas, ' darkness' (inertia), whence proceed ignorance, infatuation, delusion, mental blindness, etc.

5. The Bharata here intended must not be confounded with the young prince. He was a holy sage, the director or manager of the god's dramas, and inventor of theatrical representations in general. He wrote a work containing precepts and rules relating to every branch of dramatic writing, which appears to have been lost, but is constantly quoted by the commentators.

6. The wife of the god Brahmá. She is the goddess of speech and eloquence, patroness of the arts and sciences, and inventress of the Sanskrit language. There is a festival still held in her honour for two days, about February in every year, when no Hindu will touch a pen or write a letter. The courts are all closed accordingly.

7. Shiva is usually represented as borne on a bull; his colour, as well as that of the animal he rides, being white, to denote the purity of Justice, over which he presides. In his destroying capacity, he is characterized by the quality ' darkness,' and named Rudra, Kala, etc., when his colour is said to be purple or black. Some refer the epithet ' purple' to the colour of his throat. Self-existent, although propely a name of Brahmá, the Creator, is applied equally to Vishnu and Shiva.

8. That is, Shiva's wife, Parvatí, who was supposed to personify his energy or active power. Exemption from further transmigration, and absorption into the divine soul, was the *summum bonum* of Hindu philosophy. Compare note 3. Act II.

STAGE DIRECTIONS.

R, Right ; L, Left ; C, Centre ; R. U. E. Right upper entrance, L. U. E. Left upper entrance ; C, Door ; Centre Door.

www.ingramcontent.com/pod-product-compliance
Lightning Source LLC
Chambersburg PA
CBHW032353020726
47499CB00008B/2729